*Ame...*

# Friendship
## Survival Guide

by Marissa Moss
(and trying to be the BEST BFF, amelia)

featuring

amelia's Book of
Notes & Note
Passing

*and*

amelia's
BFF

## MORE FRIENDS!
## MORE TO READ!

SIMON & SCHUSTER BOOKS FOR YOUNG READERS
NEW YORK    LONDON    TORONTO    SYDNEY    NEW DELHI

This notebook is dedicated to Golda Laurens because I'd love to do a group project with her!

SIMON & SCHUSTER BOOKS FOR YOUNG READERS
An imprint of Simon & Schuster Children's Publishing Division
1230 Avenue of the Americas, New York, New York 10020

Amelia's Book of Notes & Notepassing
Copyright © 2006 by Marissa Moss

Amelia's BFF
Copyright © 2011 by Marissa Moss

A Paula Wiseman Book

For information about special discounts for bulk purchases, please contact Simon & Schuster Special Sales at 1-866-506-1949 or business@simonandschuster.com.
The Simon & Schuster Speakers Bureau can bring authors to your live event. For more information or to book an event, contact the Simon & Schuster Speakers Bureau at 1-866-248-3049 or visit our website at www.simonspeakers.com.

Book design by Amelia
Good with any project!

(with help from Lucy Ruth Cummins)

Part of a fascinating scientific experiment! →The text for this book is hand-lettered.

Manufactured in China 0913 SCP

2  4  6  8  10  9  7  5  3

CIP data for this book is available from the
Library of Congress.

where's the laboratory of Congress?

ISBN 978-1-4424-8304-0

These titles were previously published individually

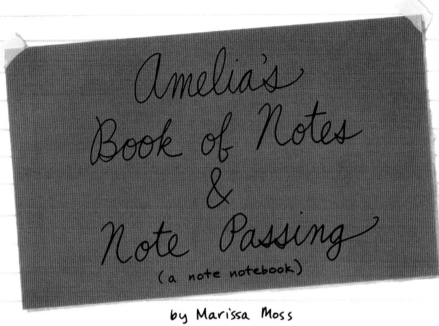

# Amelia's
# Book of Notes
# &
# Note Passing
## (a note notebook)

by Marissa Moss
(except all notably noted
and notated notes by Amelia)

I saw
this note →
when science
class started
on Monday.
It seemed
innocent enough.

**CLASS NOTICE**
Please welcome our new
student, Maxine!

It may as
well have
been
introducing
Frankenstein!
↙

Normally who cares about new students? It's their
job to figure out how to fit in, where to go, what to
do. All you have to do is be nice so they don't have a
horrible first day. I know how it feels to be the
new kid — I've done that. So of course I was polite
to Maxine. I showed her the right place in the
textbook. I smiled. Okay, I didn't give her my
extra slide when we were looking at bacteria,
but I let her have the good microscope, the one
without a crack on the lens.

And she smiled back at me. She seemed nice. But
now I'm not sure. All because of the nasty notes.

Writing and reading have been two of my favorite things
for as long as I can remember. I've always thought of paper
and pens as my friends. Not anymore. Now they're my enemies.
Enemies in the form of nasty notes. The question is <u>who</u>
made them my enemies. That's where the new girl comes

in. The ugly notes all started after she came to our
school. Besides, there's something about her I don't trust.

Here's what I know about her.

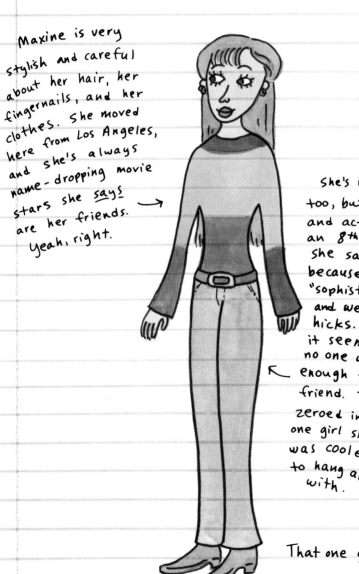

Maxine is very stylish and careful about her hair, her fingernails, and her clothes. She moved here from Los Angeles, and she's always name-dropping movie stars she _says_ are her friends. Yeah, right. →

She's in 6th grade too, but she looks and acts more like an 8th grader. She says that's because she's "sophisticated", and we're all hicks. At first it seemed like no one was good enough to be her friend. Then she zeroed in on the one girl she thought was cool enough to hang around with.

That one girl was...

Carly, my best friend →

She's cool but in a _nice_ way, not in a mean, snotty way.

Of course, Maxine would never look at me — I'm beneath her notice, like some kind of crumb on the floor. Except Carly likes me. We sit next to each other when we can. We eat lunch together. And after school we walk home together. And because Carly's so cool, a little bit of her coolness rubs off on me. That's not why I like her — besides being cool, she's smart and funny and sweet. But it's a nice bonus, since there's no way I'd be cool on my own.

Reasons why I'm NOT cool

My mom cuts my hair even though I BEG her not to! Her way of trimming bangs is to put masking tape across my forehead and chop away.

Mom doesn't let me buy clothes that look good and are in style. All she cares about are price — it has to be cheap — and what she calls "wearability" — meaning how long something will last. Unfortunately "sturdy" is NOT a nice description when it comes to clothes. And it's even WORSE for shoes.

I'm _still_ not allowed to get my ears pierced. I must be the last girl on the planet with this problem.

So I'm not surprised Maxine didn't try to be friends with me. Why should she? And I'm not surprised she'd want to be friends with Carly. Who wouldn't want that? But I am surprised that once she decided to go after Carly she didn't include me in her plans. Just the opposite.

Carly and I were eating lunch together — as usual — when Maxine came up.

"Hey, Carly," she said. "Can I sit with you?" Not "Hey, Carly, hey, Amelia." Not "Can I sit with you guys?" She was crystal clear about that.

Naturally Carly, being a nice person, was welcoming to the new girl.

"Sure, of course," she said. "So how do you like Ms. Reilly?" Since we're in 6th grade, we change classes each period and science with Ms. Reilly is one of the classes we have together.

Maxine was too busy unpacking her lunch to answer.

← sushi lined up in a beautiful box

↑ cute container of wasabi

↑ adorable container of soy sauce

It was the most elaborate lunch I've ever seen. She took an extra-long time, placing everything just so, like it was a dramatic performance and she wanted to be sure to impress Carly with her amazing, wondrous lunch.

And it worked. Carly was impressed — I could tell. She stopped chewing her sandwich and watched silently as Maxine displayed her edible treasures.

Maxine expertly picked up a sushi roll with the chopsticks.

"Would you like one?" she offered. Not to me, of course, but to Carly.

"Thanks!" Carly reached for it with her fingers. "I love sushi! You're so lucky to get that in your lunch."

My own lunch looked miserable in comparison. What could I possibly tempt Carly with?

↑
cold hot-dog sandwich—
bordering on bleecch

↑
orange —
ho hum

↑
peanut butter cookies—
okay, these are tasty, but
ordinary, nothing special

"I just love wasabi, don't you?" Maxine said, an instant expert on exotic, unpronounceable foods. "At my old school we once had a wasabi tasting to see which kind was the best."

That was my first clue that Maxine was a liar. I mean, what school would do that? And why? And do different brands of wasabi even exist here? I didn't know there was such a vast choice in Japanese food, but maybe in Los Angeles where she came from that's true. Still, it seemed highly unlikely.

But Carly believed it. And she was impressed again.

"That's so cool! You must miss your old school. We never do stuff like that here."

Maxine sighed dramatically. "Yes, I do miss it. But I'm sure there are great things about this school. You'll have to show them to me."

I was gritting my teeth so hard, my jaw ached. Couldn't Carly tell what a phony Maxine was?

"Sure!" Carly smiled. "Amelia and I would love to do that."

I wiggled my eyebrows furiously, trying to signal to Carly to count me OUT, to count herself out too.

Somehow Carly didn't get my secret eyebrow message. But I'm pretty sure Maxine did. And she didn't like what she saw.

"Amelia!" Maxine turned to me as if she'd just noticed my existence. "Such an original haircut. You really _must_ tell me where you get it done — so I can be sure NOT to go there." She laughed like it was a great joke we all could enjoy — only I didn't see anything funny about it.

But Carly did! She laughed.

Then she put her arm around me — as if THAT made it okay.

You don't want Amelia's mom to cut your hair — she's a butcher with scissors, a real public safety hazard.

I couldn't believe it! My best friend was laughing AT me!
I shrugged her arm off.

"C'mon, Amelia, don't be mad," Carly coaxed. "We always
laugh about your mom giving you haircuts. You think it's funny too!"

I didn't say anything. I couldn't with Maxine sitting there
smiling so smugly. But I was thinking it's one thing laughing
at something together with your best friend, and it's another
when someone else makes fun of you. Couldn't Carly see that?

Just then the bell rang and lunch was over — saved by the
bell! Maxine packed her stuff up quickly, especially
considering how long it took her to UNpack it.

"I guess I'll see you tomorrow. I have French now."

Carly leaped up. "So do I! I wonder if we're in the same
class."

They were. Off they went, chattering away— in French!
And off I stomped to my next class, math, with a
horrible pounding headache — not a good way to face
45 minutes of equations.

I tried to focus
on the problems in
front of me, but all
I could think of
was Carly. →

I <u>had</u> to talk to
her, to convince
her of Maxine's
phoniness before
it was too late.
↙

I could just imagine the two of them laughing at me all through French class.

All I could hear was them making fun of me — I wasn't listening to Mrs. Church at all.

Obviously I didn't know the answer to problem 17, and now I have an extra page of homework to do. I felt like Maxine was putting a curse on me. Then when I got to my locker, I knew she was hexing me. That was when I got the first note.

It looked like an innocent piece of paper, neatly folded into a → triangle.

Someone had slid it through the crack in the locker ↙ door.

Usually mail is an exciting thing. Everyone loves to get cards and letters. Packages are even better. But this note was NOT the good kind of mail. It was ugly. It was mean. It was poisonous. It said:

If this note had a face, it would be covered in warts. →

OMG! Do people still cut their hair that way?! Like there's a bowl over their head? What's WRONG with you that you go out in PUBLIC like that?! GET A CLUE!!

← The second time in ONE day my hair was insulted. I wished I was BALD!

I read it and felt a sour stab in my stomach. I couldn't read it twice. I couldn't even examine it for clues about who wrote it. I had to throw it away as fast as possible.

It was so toxic, it made the whole trash can steam with its putrid stench. →

I threw the orange from my lunch on top of it, trying to sink it. I wanted it far, far away.

Even with the note gone, I was so upset, I was shaking. Who hated me so much they would write such mean words? I couldn't imagine. Then I heard a laugh — two laughs. It was Maxine and Carly walking down the hall. Could Maxine have slipped the note into my locker? When would she have had time? Wouldn't Carly have seen her do it? It didn't seem possible, but who else could it be? After all, she'd made that nasty remark about my haircut. And could it be a coincidence — new girl arrives, new nasty note appears? It had to be Maxine — evil, mean Maxine!

I closed my locker and walked toward them, pretending nothing was wrong.

I was trying so hard to look normal, my face felt stiff. →

Hey, Carly. Hey, Maxine. Sounds like French was a lot of fun.

Carly grinned. "You should have heard Maxine! She asked the teacher what 'les fesses' means, and he got all embarrassed. It was a crack-up! Too bad we don't all have French together."

I nodded. I had Mr. LePoivre for French too, but not the same period as Carly. "Ha, ha, that's funny," I said, NOT laughing. Omar had asked the same question in my class last week. So "les fesses" meant ω — behind, tush, bum. So what? That was hilarious?

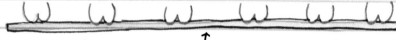

a row of fesses on a bench — or lots of ω's

"So, Carly," I went on. "You're coming over today after school, right?"

Carly stopped laughing. "Oh, I forgot about that. Maxine invited me to her house." She looked at Maxine as if she was waiting for Maxine to ask me over too.

Maxine looked at a spot above my head. "I'd invite you, Amelia, but my mom said I could only have one person over today."

I turned to follow Maxine's gaze. Since she was talking to the bulletin board behind me, maybe it would answer her. After a few minutes it seemed clear the bulletin board would not cooperate, so I had to say something.

"That's okay," I lied. I faced Carly. "You go without me."

"Okay." Carly didn't look at all upset. "See you later then."

Byeeeee!

↑
Maxine drew out the "eeee" in "Bye" so it sounded like there were two syllables. Just that little thing made her sound very happy to leave me behind. Just that little thing made me miserable.

Maxine looked like she'd gotten her way. A smug, self-satisfied smirk twitched on her face. I wanted to punch that smile right off of her, but all I could do was get my books and head to English.

After school I waited for Carly at our usual place, but she never showed up. I guess she'd gone right home with Maxine. So I walked home alone.

The day was gray and cold, but not as gray and cold as I felt inside. →

It was one of the worst days of my life.

As I passed by houses, all cheery and lit up like whoever lived there was happy, I thought about all the bad things that had happened to me in my entire life. I wondered how today measured up against those other bad days.

Some things are bad but in a small, annoying way, like burnt toast, a pebble in your shoe, a pop quiz. Other things are bad in a BIG way, like Cleo, my awful sister, like the first time I had an asthma attack, like my dad leaving when I was just a baby. I wasn't sure where today fit in, but it seemed pretty bad.

small bad stuff
↓

↑
mosquito bite

cold hot-dog sandwich

sniff,
sniff
↑
a stuffy nose

# BIG BAD STUFF
↓

I get an evil note _
badness: 10
↓

↑
My sister, Cleo, sits next to me on the bus for the field trip and pukes — badness: 6

Carly abandons me for Maxine _
↑
badness: 10

I waited for Carly to call that night, but she never did. A bad day was turning into a bad night. I had horrible dreams.

In one dream Carly and Maxine were best friends and I was completely shut out. I followed them around school, hoping for a chance to join in, but it never happened. I was all alone, a fate worse than death in middle school.

When I woke up, I worried that my dream was coming true. I wanted to wear something so cool that Carly would like me again, but there were two problems with that — one, I didn't _own_ anything cool, and two, Carly had never been the type to care about stuff like that. That's why she was my friend in the first place. And anyway, just because she'd gone over to Maxine's house didn't mean she didn't like me anymore. But if _I_ don't like Maxine, then she can't either or she's breaking one of the rules of best-friendness — the enemy of my friend is MY enemy. I had to remind Carly of that!

So I wore what I normally wear and went to school. Luckily PE was first period and that's a class I have with Carly — WITHOUT Maxine.

When I saw Carly, I tried to act like my usual self.

"Hey," I said.

"Hey," she said.

"How was Maxine's?" I asked.

"Okay," she answered.

I wasn't sure, but something seemed just a little bit off. Was I imagining it or was Carly not as friendly as usual?

"So how about today?" I asked.

"Today what?" Carly looked blank.

"Today after school. You're coming over, right?"

"Um, oh, that." Carly was careful not to look me in the eye. "I don't think that'll work today — maybe later."

Carly didn't say she had plans, but I got the feeling she definitely did. Only <u>not</u> with me — with Maxine.

Then it was time for basketball and we couldn't talk much, but that was okay because by the end of the period, we were our old selves again, joking and laughing.

I'm terrible at sports, especially basketball, where being short (like me) really matters, but it was fun anyway to run around the court, to practice dribbling and free shots. As our muscles loosened up, so did we, and I knew Carly was my best friend again.

I wanted that feeling to last all day, but what would happen when we went to science? What would happen when Maxine was around?

Lucky for me, Maxine was late to class, so Carly and I sat next to each other. While the teacher was taking attendance, Carly passed me a note.

It was carefully folded into a triangle, like the other evil note.

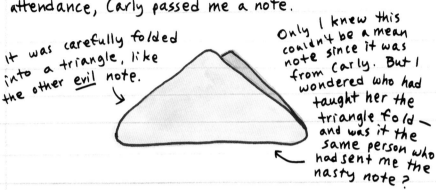

Only I knew this couldn't be a mean note since it was from Carly. But I wondered who had taught her the triangle fold — and was it the same person who had sent me the nasty note?

I quietly unfolded the note on my lap under the desk, so the teacher couldn't tell what I was doing. But even though I could see it, I couldn't read the note — it was a jumble of letters, nonsense words.

UIJT JT JO DPEF. IFSF JT UIF LFZ. XSJUF UIF BMQIBCFU JO B DJSDMF. HP POE MFUUFS UP UIF SJHIU PG UIF MFUUFS ZPV XBOU BOE VTF UIBU OFJHICPS MFUUFS JOTUFBE. USZ JU BOE TFF IPX FBTZ JU JT UP VTF!
DBSMZ

Carly looked over at me to see if I had figured it out. I shook my head. Was this Maxine's code? Something she invented? I looked at Maxine, but she was busy finding her homework to hand in. She wasn't paying attention to me or Carly. I stared at the note again, trying to make sense of it. The last five letters, D B S M Z, were trying to tell me something. Then I remembered that's how Carly used to sign her name — I had it! I knew the code! I tried my idea and it worked. This is what the note translated to:

THIS IS IN CODE. HERE IS THE KEY. WRITE THE ALPHABET IN A CIRCLE. GO ONE LETTER TO THE RIGHT OF THE LETTER YOU WANT AND USE THAT NEIGHBOR LETTER INSTEAD. TRY IT AND SEE HOW EASY IT IS TO USE!

CARLY

Carly was grinning at me — she could tell I'd solved it.

I smiled back. Of course she was still my friend! No way Maxine could steal her away!

I wanted to send a note back to her right away. But I had to be discreet. If Ms. Reilly catches you passing notes, it means DETENTION — I didn't want that.

Good thing I can write sorta neatly without even looking at the paper. I did the best I could, folded my note into a tiny rectangle, and kicked it on the floor toward Carly's foot. Here's what I wrote:

```
J MPWF ZPVS DPEF. J IBWF BO JEFB IPX
UP NBLF JU FWFO USJDLJFS. PO FBDI EBZ XF
TLJQ POF NPSF MFUUFS TP VIF DPEF
DFBOHFT. USZ VIJT TFOUFODF:
    AQW HKIWTGF KV QWV!
        COGNKC
```

What I really wanted to say was how glad I was to have her for a friend, but that seemed a little mushy for a note. Anyway, I didn't need to say it. I was smiling so much, I was sure Carly could tell what I was thinking.

Carly was looking at me, waiting for a chance to pick up the note, when Maxine accidentally on purpose dropped her pencil. It rolled right next to the note! Maxine got up and bent over to pick up the pencil — and the note, too. Except Carly was quicker and she stepped on it before Maxine could grab it. She almost stepped on Maxine's fingers!

I glared at Maxine. She knew that note wasn't for her! What was she, anyway, some kind of mail thief? The rest of class took forever — the slowest 20 minutes of my life. Finally the bell rang, and Carly snatched up the note before she gathered up her stuff.

I waited for her in the hall. Only when she came out, Maxine was with her!

Why did you try to grab Carly's note? That wasn't for you!

How was I supposed to know that? I didn't see her name on it or anything.

I was furious!

she was infuriatingly calm! ↗

"It was just a simple misunderstanding," Carly said. "No harm done. And Maxine apologized to me."

"Well, she didn't apologize to _me_!" I said. I was FURIOUS at Carly, too. How could she stand up for Maxine? That was breaking another rule of best-friendness.

"Oh, Amelia, I'm so, _so_ sooooorry," Maxine drawled, making it perfectly clear she wasn't sorry at all.

"See — that's that!" Carly grabbed my arm and pulled me down the hall. "Let's go eat lunch!"

Maxine slipped her arm around Carly's other arm. "Yes, let's."

I wanted to talk to Carly and remind her how friends are SUPPOSED to act. I wanted to talk with her IN PRIVATE. Most of all, I wanted Carly to be my friend again, not some evil traitor. Instead I was stuck with Maxine eating her fabulous lunch of Chinese chicken salad.

I concentrated on chewing my fish-stick sandwich (another of mom's gross lunch specialties) until Maxine got up to throw away her trash. I only had a minute, but I used it as best I could.

What's up with you and Maxine? I need to talk to you — WITHOUT her around.

Sure, no problem. I'll walk home with you, okay?

I was so relieved. Carly was still my friend. She hadn't gone over to the dark side after all. But then Maxine came back, sat down next to Carly, and whispered something in her ear.

Carly laughed. I frowned. I mean, how RUDE! I tried to act like I didn't care.

How nice — a little humor for dessert is so pleasant.

Perhaps you could share the cause for your merriment, allow the laughter to spread.

I don't think I fooled anyone.

"Hah!" Maxine barked. "Could you say that again in plain English? You must be speaking some strange kind of dialect."

"Really?" I arched an eyebrow. "I'm sure Carly understood me. Didn't you, Carly?"

Carly looked embarrassed. She knew just how obnoxious Maxine was being. I waited for her to stick up for me. I waited a <u>loooooong</u> minute. Then the bell rang and it was time for class. Lucky for Carly because she didn't have to say anything. Lucky for me because I didn't have to see Carly NOT stand by me. Maybe she would have. Now I'd never know.

"See you after school," I said.

"Yeah." Carly nodded. She still looked embarrassed.

"Ta-ta!" Maxine said, wiggling her fingers. I couldn't help it. Just her voice, just the way she moved her fingers — I HATED HER!

I couldn't make a voodoo doll of Maxine, so I did the next best thing. I drew one. When I get home, I can stick it with real pins, but for now I can label what curses will happen when that part of the body is poked. It was very satisfying.

Real voodoo dolls are shapeless lumps.

My paper one was much more realistic.

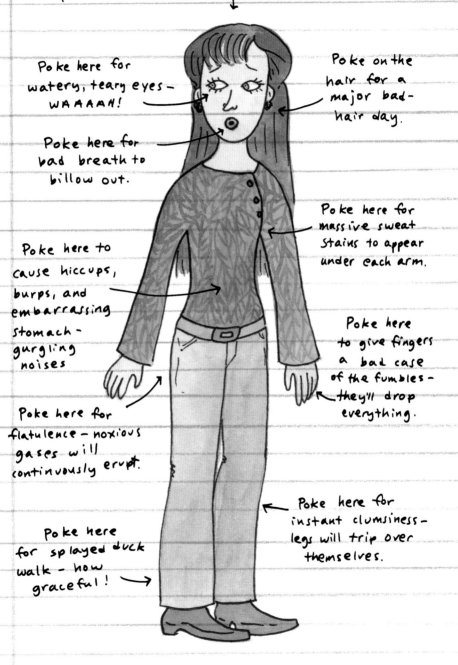

Just drawing the voodoo doll made me feel MUCH better. Then I got to my locker and felt MUCH worse. There was another note in it — even nastier than the first one.

It was so foul, I could barely stand to touch it. I threw it away as fast as I could. →

Amelia—
Take a bath! You're polluting the whole cafeteria. Even Sloppy Joes can't cover your stink!

I took deep breaths trying to calm myself. Who could hate me that much? It <u>had</u> to be Maxine. I hated her, so she must hate me. But to be <u>that</u> vicious? I would never say those things to anyone, no matter how much I detested them. Could it really be Maxine? I didn't know what to think. I had to see Carly. I had to tell her about the notes. She'd know what to do. She always did.

I was relieved to see her waiting for me after school. →

I was afraid she'd change her mind and go home with Maxine again, but there she was, trustworthy as ever. And NO Maxine in sight.

Except something felt a little bit off. I couldn't say exactly what. Carly looked the same. She acted the same. She sounded the same. Only she didn't. I began to wonder if she was a Carly clone, a copy substituting for the real thing.

I waited to see what would happen. She brought up Maxine first.

"Um, sorry about that thing back at lunch," Carly said, studying the sidewalk. At last — she apologized. The rules of best-friendness still held. Or did they? Something was still off.

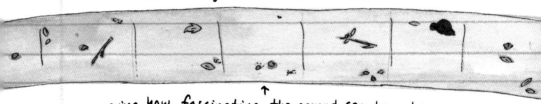

It's amazing how fascinating the ground can be when you want to avoid looking at someone. All I saw were pebbles, twigs, a leaf or two, dog poop to be avoided, but Carly kept her eyes glued to the sidewalk as if the mystery of the universe was written there.

I was going to say something, to ask what was going on with Maxine, to tell Carly about the mean notes, when I noticed something on the sidewalk. All I could tell was that it was a piece of crumpled-up binder paper, but it seemed like a message from the universe. I picked it up and smoothed it out. It could have been a page of homework or part of a report. But it wasn't. It was a note.

2: Alexa

Look, u need to drop it. Vanessa
is making you do this. Look, Alexa,
u were nice and this one girl made
u change. I suggest u leave her
because she is bad for you. She
just wants u to be hurt. If u
don't change, I'm never speaking
to u.

Jasmine

I read it out loud to Carly. The note was so true, it
was creepy! Only I should have written it, not Jasmine. And
it should be to Carly, not Alexa. And instead of Vanessa,
it should say Maxine.

I stared at Carly. "I think this note's for you."

She laughed nervously. "Come on, Amelia, you just found
that on the ground. It's to some girl named Alexa who
probably dropped it on purpose because it was none of
Jasmine's business."

"Are you saying it's none of my business?" I asked.

"Amelia! I'm talking about the note. What are you talking about?"

"You," I said. "And Maxine. She's the one who's bad for you. And you're the one who's changed."

"What do you mean? You're just mad because of the whispering at lunch. Okay, I admit that was rude, but bad manners doesn't make someone evil. It was a mistake, that's all." Carly still wasn't looking at me. Now she was looking up at the power lines.

"Don't you wonder who throws shoes up there and why they do it?" she asked.

"Don't change the subject!" I snapped.

"Come on, Amelia, this is the kind of thing we talk about. It's why I like you so much — you notice stuff like that. It's true I like Maxine, but I'll always like you, too."

I sighed. Carly still liked me. But was she my best friend? Could she be my best friend and still like Maxine? I shook my head. It didn't work that way. She couldn't like both me and Maxine. The universe would implode.

"I'm not wondering about shoes right now," I said. "I'm wondering about notes. Mean notes."

Carly looked at me — finally. "You mean the note Maxine tried to take?"

"That was mean of her. But the note wasn't mean."

She was looking at me, not up or down, so I told her about the mean notes stuck in my locker.

"Maybe they weren't meant for you," Carly said. "Like the note you just found on the sidewalk."

"What? The notes had my name on them!"

Carly shrugged. "Maybe they got the wrong Amelia's locker."

I shook my head. "So you don't think Maxine did it?"

Carly looked shocked. "Maxine! Why her? Of course not!"

I didn't know why her, but who else could it be? Can people hate you for no good reason?

Just then a piece of paper fluttered by.

It looked like another note. Suddenly I was seeing notes everywhere. → ← I grabbed it and read it out loud.

Thanks for parking so close! Next time leave a can opener so I can get my car out. Jerks like you should take the bus!

Carly laughed. "Well, that's a nasty note and it's clearly not meant for you. Or me," she added.

"No!" I laughed too. "Though it sounds like something Cleo would write once she starts driving — and parking."

Carly looped her arm through mine. "Listen, the only notes meant for you are the ones I send you, and we have our own secret code so no one else can understand them."

It was like the good old days walking with Carly. We didn't talk about Maxine at all and I liked it that way.

↓

We talked about our code and ways to make it trickier. I was thinking about all the different kinds of notes there are in the world — the kinds left on cars, on doors, in lockers, on refrigerators, in books, the kind you pass in school, and the kind you bring to school after you've been out sick. And the kind you find on the sidewalk, lost notes finding a new home with someone else, taking on a new meaning like some sort of message from the universe.

Once I started looking, I saw notes everywhere! It seemed like people lost notes constantly. Maybe the ones I found in my locker really were a mistake. Maybe they were simply lost notes.

When Carly saw I was picking up scraps of paper to see if there was anything interesting, she started doing it too. Together we found:

a paper doll

a school photo

a ticket stub

Admit One

a shopping list —
I'm sure this was an old person's list. Who else buys this stuff?

baloney
string
horseradish
prunes
buttermilk
light bulbs
butter pecan ice cream

a playing card

ARI—
I COULDN'T WAIT ANY LONGER. HAD TO GO. CALL ME. MIKE

a note

Carly helped me start a scrapbook with the notes we found. Then I added the one she'd passed to me in class and a key that I made so it would be easier to solve our code.

With the letters in an oval like this, it's easier to see which letter you need to go to when you're skipping a space.

A B C D E F G H I J K L M N O P Q R S T U V W X Y Z

Carly said she got the idea for this code from her dad. He had a decoder ring like this when he was a kid, only there were two alphabets, one around the other, so you could dial the ring to solve the code.

It was good to have a project to work on together. It helped wash out the bad taste of Maxine and the nasty notes. But then something happened that brought it all back, uglier than ever.

Carly noticed a shirt on my bed.

"Ugh, Amelia, you still have this old thing? Isn't it time to throw it away or give it to Goodwill?"

"Why?" I asked. "I just wore it the other day."

"I know!" Carly groaned. "That's why you need to get rid of it. Maxine said..."

Just those two words — "Maxine said" — they were like a kick in the stomach.

"Maxine said what? WHAT?!" I yelled. "I knew she hated me! And you don't stick up for me! That's what friends do, remember! That's why you can't like her!"

"She does not!" Carly looked mad, but I felt madder. "She simply said, she said..." Carly sighed, then plowed on. "She said you look like a dork in this shirt. It's so '70s."

"Isn't that a good thing? Aren't the '70s in again?" I asked.

"No!" snapped Carly. "It's a _bad_ thing. The '70s are a decade that should be erased in terms of style. Maxine's right — you have no sense of fashion."

I screamed, "MAXINE!! Who cares what SHE says?! I've ALWAYS dressed like this — I've worn this shirt a million times. And you've never cared before. You're supposed to stick up for me, to tell Maxine to SHOVE IT! That's what best friends DO! Now you're sticking up for MAXINE!!!"

I screeched so loudly, my throat felt ragged. Carly looked at me coldly.

"I think I'd better go," she said. "I should have gone to Maxine's house. _She_ doesn't shriek at me."

I wadded up the dork shirt and flung it at Carly. "Go, then! And give this shirt to Maxine when you see her!'"

Carly stepped over the shirt like it was a pool of poison. She didn't look back. She didn't say good-bye. By the time I went to bed, she still hadn't called to apologize.

It was our worst fight ever.

Part of me felt satisfied because yes, Maxine <u>was</u> as bad as I suspected, telling Carly mean things about me. But most of me was miserable because Carly actually believed the horrible things. I was so upset, I couldn't sleep. Finally I got up and wrote a story. That calmed me down so I could fall asleep.

### The Nasty Notes

One day a girl found a nasty note on her pillow.

> YOU HAVE TERRIBLE BREATH!
> HAVEN'T YOU EVER HEARD OF
> BRUSHING YOUR TEETH!?

Of course, the girl <u>did</u> brush her teeth and she knew the note wasn't true. Still, it hurt that someone could even think she didn't practice good oral hygiene. She actually began to doubt whether she'd brushed her teeth that morning and hurried to brush again.

The harder the girl brushed, the more the note bothered her. →

And the more the note bothered her, the harder she brushed. ↙

The girl's teeth were sparkling, but the next day there was another note.

> YOUR BREATH SMELLS LIKE YOU CHEW FISH-EYE GUM! DO SOMETHING OR I'LL REPORT YOU AS A FRESH AIR HAZARD TO THE ENVIRONMENTAL PROTECTION AGENCY! NOW!!

The girl felt horrible. After school she rushed off to buy mouthwash and mints. But no matter how much she gargled or how many mints she sucked, the note still made her feel terrible.

The next day she found a third note slipped under her bedroom door. It said:

> I CAN'T STAND IT ANYMORE! STOP BREATHING THROUGH YOUR MOUTH — YOU'RE POLLUTING THE WHOLE WORLD!

The girl felt so awful, she crumpled on the floor and started to cry. "But I <u>do</u> breathe out my nose!" she sobbed. "And my breath isn't bad — at least not worse than anyone else's. Why is someone being so mean to me?"

Her brother heard her crying and came into her room to see what was wrong. She showed him the notes.

"Did you write these?" she asked. "Is this some kind of prank?"

The boy shook his head. "I didn't write them, but I think I know who did. Wait here." He went into his room and came back with a wooden box.

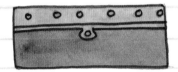

He unlatched the lid and carefully opened it.

Huddled in a corner was a small furry creature with sharp claws and fangs.

All around it were pieces of paper with words scrawled on them.

The girl reached into the box and snatched up one of the pieces of paper. It said: "I KNOW WHO FARTED IN CLASS TODAY! CAN'T YOU CONTROL YOURSELF?!"

"What is this?" she asked, dropping the paper quickly.

"I'm not sure," admitted her brother. "I found it in the attic and it demanded paper and pencils. When I opened the box to check on it, it had written all these mean notes."

"I guess it can escape the box," the boy continued. "It must have left those notes for you to find. I don't know why it's like that."

"Then why don't you get rid of it?" the girl asked.

The boy slammed the lid shut. "It's cool! No one else has one! I want to keep it. Okay, it's mean, but only with words."

"That's the <u>worst</u> kind of meanness," said the girl. "But fine, you keep it. At least now I can ignore the notes."

But the next day there was no new note. Nor the day after that. Finally the girl asked her brother what happened to his creature — was it okay?

"I got rid of it," said the boy. "I took it to school and let it out in the soccer field."

"Why? I thought you liked it." The girl was surprised.

"I did," the boy said, "until it started hiding nasty notes for me."

CAN'T YOU SEE THE GROSS GREEN FILM ON YOUR TEETH? EVERYONE ELSE CAN! DO SOMETHING ABOUT IT OR I'LL CALL THE UGLY POLICE !!

The girl laughed and gave her brother a hug. And neither of them got a nasty note again.

But the other kids in school had some unpleasant surprises.

**The End**

In the morning I felt better until it was time for science. I couldn't face seeing Carly and Maxine together, even though I'd been careful to wear something I knew Carly would approve of.

She'd given me this shirt for my birthday last year, so it <u>had</u> to be okay. →

I hoped one cool shirt could make up for a bad haircut and bad shoes.

I got to class as late as I could without getting marked tardy. I didn't want any awkward time sitting next to Carly and NOT talking to each other. I slipped into my seat and tried not to look at her, but I couldn't help it — I saw Carly and Maxine exchange a glance that said "Ignore her!"

That was fine with me because I was ignoring <u>them</u> first. At least I did until Maxine kicked a note over to Carly. Too bad it ended up closer to my chair than to Carly's.

I almost stomped my foot over the note, but I didn't. I couldn't be a Maxine. Instead I stared straight ahead while Carly picked up the note and read it. I could feel the searing heat of Maxine glaring at me, but I didn't look at her. I just kept my eyes on the blackboard and read the same sentence about kinetic energy 36 times.

When the bell rang, Carly and Maxine got up together without one glance at me. At the door I thought Carly was going to turn around and wave to me. I thought she was going to rush over and apologize and promise never to talk to Maxine again. She didn't. She just flicked a paper into the trash and left.

I wanted to stick out my tongue and say "Nyah, nyah, who wants you anyway?" But I'm in the 6th grade now. I can't act like a baby, even though sometimes it's VERY tempting.

what I wanted to do. →

NYAH, NYAH!

Hmmm... interesting.

what I did do. ←

I waited until I was sure they had left — and so had everyone else, even Ms. Reilly. Then I went over to the trash can and looked for the paper Carly had dropped.

I couldn't believe it — it was the note and it was in code, our code! Carly must have told Maxine how to solve it. She'd shared our secrets! I tried to calm myself down so I could read what it said, but I was so upset over Carly's betrayal, I almost didn't care what the note said. The note being in code already told me devastating news — Carly was treating Maxine like a best friend, her new best friend.

OHWV HDW OXQFK EHKLQG WKH
JBP. L ZDQW WR PDNH VXUH
DPHOLD GRHVQW ILQG XV.
HDWLQJ ZLWK KHU ZRXOG
VSRLO PB DSSHWLWH!

I tried skipping one letter, but that didn't work. Skipping two didn't work either, and I began to worry that maybe they had their own code, one I didn't know at all. Then I tried skipping three letters, and finally the note made sense: "Let's eat lunch behind the gym. I want to make sure Amelia doesn't find us. Eating with her will spoil my appetite!"

My stomach pitched — I felt queasy and clammy like when I had the flu. What should I do? Confront them? Avoid them?

Maybe the best thing to do was to eat lunch by myself
wherever I wanted to go. If they were there, fine. If not, that
was okay too. I wasn't eager to talk to the two of them anyway.

On the way to the cafeteria I found three notes. I wished
they were for me, but they weren't. The only notes I got
these days were bad ones.

Cheryl,
hey, wassup?
Wanna head
downtown today
after school?

Dee —
Did u see how M. looked
at me?! I know he likes
me!!! ♡♡♡ ♡ ♡ 4EVER!
K.

Yes, it is SO true! I know
becuz he told me himself.
This is NO rumor!

I sat by myself and ate my leftover cold spaghetti
(Mom's bad lunch ideas strike again!). Now I not only had
icky food, I had no one to eat it with, making it taste
even worse. It's dangerous to eat by yourself in middle
school. You need to belong somewhere.

# Perils of Lunch Alone

Sitting by yourself labels you a Loser, so no one comes to sit next to you, so you look like a Loser, so...

Any food thrown in a food fight ALWAYS finds its way to those poor kids doomed to eat by themselves— SPLAT!

Bullies looking for a victim to pick on naturally zero in on defenseless solitary eaters. With no friends to shield them, they are complete sitting ducks, adding insult to injury (and injury to insult).

QUACK!

Besides the social trauma, there's no one to trade your apple with, no one to share their candy bar with you, no one to feel sorry for the miserable lunch your mom packed so they give you some of theirs. You're doomed to eat only food from home — bleecch!

There's an unspoken ranking of everyone, and once you sink to the bottom of the pile, it's almost impossible to raise yourself up. Where would I fit without Carly?

On the top
↓

Really cool people who do the knowing and don't need to be known by anyone.

Cool people who are known by the really cool people.

↑
With Carly, I'm almost here.

The mass of other people — some nice, some bad, some boring, some interesting, but not cool, though they can have cool friends (really this is below the two cool groups on the side).

↑
Without Carly, I'm here.

Cool people who are nice and know other cool people, which adds to their coolness.

Library people— people with no friends, so they hang out in the library to feel safe.

Hallway lurkers — need I say more?

Jocks — people who play soccer or basketball at lunch.

Gamers and nerds— people who only like each other and are NOT cool in any way, shape, or form.

Smelly people — no one likes them or can even stand to be near them.

Jerks— people no one likes.

Total losers — worse even than smelly people.

I wondered what group Carly and Maxine belonged in — one for snarky, mean people and traitorous friends? I didn't see them anywhere. But I did find another note.

Don't forget to return library book!!!

Maybe it was a sign that I should go to the library — though I didn't want to become a lonely library person. Maybe it was a sign that I had no idea what to do to get Carly back and was desperate enough to listen to random notes. Maybe it was both. Anyway, I was desperate enough to try anything. So I went to the library.

And there was Carly! With no Maxine in sight! I hadn't thought about what I should say, but I couldn't miss the opportunity.

"Listen, I'm sorry about yesterday," I said, rushing up to her. "I just felt bad that it seemed like you were picking Maxine over me. I knew you wouldn't do that." I wanted us to be friends again. I wanted Carly to write notes to me, in our own secret code that no one else knew. I wanted Maxine to move back to her old house and old school and leave us alone.

I waited for Carly to say something, to be her old self again.

"Maybe I am," she said after a horribly long silence.

"Maybe you are what?" I asked.

"Maybe I am choosing Maxine over you. You're the one who forced me to decide. I thought you could both be my friends. I guess I was wrong."

"But we can!" I squeaked, terrified. "I'm not making you pick —
it's Maxine. She's the one telling awful lies about me!"

"Well, look who's here. She must have sniffed you out, Carly."
Maxine walked up. She must have been in the bathroom. Too bad
she didn't have diarrhea and would have to spend the rest of
lunch there. "Has Amelia tracked you down for some more of her
famous insults?"

"I didn't track anyone down." I tried not to yell, to keep my
voice calm. "And I'm NOT insulting Carly."

"Oh? You're insulting me instead?" Maxine shrugged. "Figures."
My face felt hot and red. "I did not!" I sputtered.

"Forget it, Amelia," Carly said softly. She scooped her books
up into her backpack. "Gotta go."

I watched them walk out of the library together. I felt
as brittle as glass, ready to shatter.

When I'd collected myself and could move again, I headed to my locker. I thought about Carly's last words. She hadn't sounded angry, just sad. Maybe we could still be friends. We'd fought before and made up. That's what friends do. But we'd never had such a horrible fight and there'd never been someone like Maxine involved before. I didn't know what to think — or what to do.

It didn't seem like the day could get any worse. Yet amazingly enough, it did. Another vicious note was waiting in my locker.

It was like a ticking → time bomb....

Can you get any more pathetic? Where do you get your clothes anyway, Goodwill? _Bad will?_

... made of paper and highly explosive ← words.

I didn't want to read it, but I couldn't stop myself. I crumpled up the paper with trembling hands and threw it away before I could read it again. I didn't want the ugly words to sink in.

The evil creature from my story had struck again! →

Hee, hee, hee!

And that wasn't the end of the day — I still had English to face — my worst class with my worst teacher, the dreaded Mr. Lambaste. If he was mean to me on today of all days, I'd melt into a puddle on the floor. I was used to him being a jerk — and normally as soon as I set foot into his class, I wore mental armor, a shield to ward off his sharp words. Today I was too fragile to muster up my usual toughness.

I looked like this...

...but felt like this.

I was wearing clothes, but I still felt like I was naked, like a baby bird before it grows feathers to protect its tender skin.

Luckily Mr. L. ignored me, so I didn't have to ward off any nasty comments or mean remarks. In fact, he didn't insult anyone today, he was too excited about the Shakespeare play we were starting to read, Othello. At first I was too busy feeling sorry for myself to pay much attention to what Mr. L. was saying. But when he described the story, especially the part about Iago, I got really interested. For a play that was written 5 centuries ago, it sounded eerily like my life! In the play, Othello, a black officer in the Venetian navy, is married to Desdemona, a white woman. They're very much in love until Iago, who is Othello's righthand man, decides to ruin his commander.

Iago is intensely jealous of Othello and wants to destroy him, so he starts a vicious rumor that Desdemona is unfaithful. He whispers mean hints to Othello, poisoning his ear with ugly lies. And Othello believes him, putting more faith in Iago's nasty words than in honest Desdemona. Othello is driven into such a jealous rage, he ends up killing the woman he loves. It's a very sad story. And very powerful because it shows that words _can_ hurt — they can even kill.

Of course, Carly wouldn't hurt a fly. But Maxine is a snake like Iago, hissing nasty things into Carly's ear, trying to convince her I'm not a good friend. And it's working!

At least in the play Othello _does_ learn that Iago has been lying all along, only it's too late. Desdemona is dead. That's it — the only solution is to prove to Carly that Maxine's an evil liar!

Except she's more evil than a liar. I _do_ have a bad haircut. I _do_ wear lame clothes. But I'm still a good person and Carly always saw that before. I needed to show Carly how _mean_ Maxine is. If only I had proof that she's the one leaving me the nasty notes.

HELP!

How could I trap her? I needed a giant, sticky web.

# Possible Locker Alarms and Traps

**Paint Marker**

The paint? Um, this is part of my costume. I'm a pea in "The Princess and the Pea."

Notes? What notes? Wasn't me.

**Smell Catcher**

Yap, yap!

Paint is detonated from spray can when paper is slipped into locker, marking person who did it so all can see.

Small dog lives in locker — when note is pushed in, dog catches scent of hand doing the pushing. When dog is let out of locker, he follows his nose to track down the culprit (unless cafeteria odors distract him).

**Siren Alarm**

WEE-OOH WEE-OOH WEE-OOH!

Don't shoot!

My hands are up!

**Glue Grabber**

Alarm is triggered by paper touching locker — loud noise and flashing lights stun note writer into submission.

Area in front of locker is covered with a special glue that is activated ONLY when slits in locker door are touched (like by a note going through them). When that happens, the glue becomes SUPERSTICKY, forcing culprit to leave shoes behind in order to escape.

Naturally Carly didn't walk home with me, but I called her as soon as I could.

> Carly, let me explain something.

> Amelia, please, don't bother. I think we need a break from each other, maybe a week, while we both sort things out.

> A week?! Why so long? And what are we sorting out? You're my best friend, and I'm sorry I hurt your feelings. But I <u>have</u> to warn you not to trust Maxine.

> Funny, she says the same thing about YOU. Who am I supposed to believe?

Me! I wanted to yell - believe <u>me</u>! But it was too late. Carly had already hung up. She just needs more time, I told myself. Tomorrow she'll be her old self again, and it will be like this past week never even happened. At least that's what I hoped (along with Maxine falling into a ditch and never being seen again).

A week seemed like a looong time. There was only one thing to do - write to Nadia, my best friend before I moved away. Even far away, we were still close and whenever I didn't know what to do about something, she helped me see my choices more clearly. It might take a while to hear back from her since Mom says it's too expensive to call, but I felt better just writing to her.

Dear Nadia,
 HELP! There's a new girl at school and she's saying mean things about me to my friend, Carly, because she wants to have Carly all to herself. The worst part is, Carly actually listens to the new girl and that changes how she sees me, how she feels about me. Short of poisoning this creepy new kid, WHAT CAN I DO? *Yours till the heart beats,* amelia

Nadia Kurz
61 South St.
Barton, CA
91010

Maybe I could write nasty notes about Maxine and leave them where Carly would find them. After all, since she was saying ugly stuff about me, I should return the favor. Hmmm...what should I write? I wasn't sure if I would actually <u>do</u> anything with my mean notes, but it felt good making them. Even if no one else ever saw them, putting the words on paper got some of the Maxine poison out of my system.

Writing the notes reminded me of the time we went on vacation and my sister, Cleo, and I thought it would be funny to leave notes in the dresser drawers at the hotel we stayed in.

We wrote things like:
↓

Didn't your mother teach you to fold your underwear?

No dirty, smelly socks here, please!

In case of fire, remove all flammable pajamas first.

This is MY drawer — you can use the OTHER drawer.

We got the idea from the toilet, which was wrapped in a big note of its own.

Sanitized for your prote

↑

Don't you feel safe knowing your toilet is carefully wrapped? All my life, notes have been good things — funny or important or informative. Now I know they can be bad, too. I just had to make them work for me, not against me.

I decided to write a note after all — to Carly, not to Maxine. I started to put it in code, but it seemed too important to risk it not being solved right.

This is what I wrote: ↓

Carly —
   I'm writing you a note because this whole problem started with notes and maybe that's how it can end. I'm afraid that Maxine says mean things about me that make you not like me. It's like she's pouring poison in your ear — not to hurt y<u>ou</u>, but to poison how you feel about me, to make you not want to be my friend anymore. So I'll admit right now that yes, I'm not as cool as you. I have a bad haircut and wear stupid clothes, but that didn't used to matter to you. You liked the way I saw things, my sense of humor. Who else can talk to you about why shoes are hung on telephone wires? Who else wonders why number threes are jolly and fives are bossy?
   I miss you, Carly. I want to be your friend 4ever.
                                                    amelia

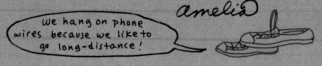
We hang on phone wires because we like to go long-distance!

I slipped the note into Carly's locker before school started. I was so nervous waiting for her to read it, I couldn't focus at all in math. The numbers ran all over the place on my worksheet and I couldn't get them to behave at all.

Then it was time for science, my first class with Carly. I got there before she did and sat down, pretending to read. I didn't have to see or hear her to know when she came into the classroom. The air felt different as soon as she stepped in. I wanted to jump up and hug her, but I kept my eyes glued to the page, holding my breath, waiting to see what would happen.

Since I wasn't looking at her, I couldn't tell if she even glanced at me on the way to her desk. I heard the rustle of her backpack as she passed by and had a clear view of her shoes, but that was it. Except when I looked up, I noticed a small square of neatly-folded paper on the corner of my desk. A note! Carly had left me a note! I grabbed it and stuck it in my pocket. I couldn't follow Ms. Reilly at all as she explained something about earthquakes. I felt like I had an earthquake in my pocket — a seismic shift in my friendship with Carly. I hoped it was a good kind of jolt, a push back together again instead of a widening of the rift between us.

I snuck peeks at Carly the whole period, but I couldn't tell what she was thinking. All I could see was that she wasn't looking at me and that seemed a bad sign.

When the bell rang, she bolted out of her seat without glancing at me — or Maxine. I didn't try to follow her. I needed to read her note first. Then I'd know what to do.

I almost said something to Maxine on my way out, but I didn't. She was studying her fingernails, trying hard to avoid noticing me. It seemed cruel to remind her of my existence.

I found a quiet corner outside the cafeteria (well, as quiet as it can get with clanking trays, clattering silverware, yelling kids, and tromping feet only a hallway away). I took out Carly's note.

Unfolding and reading it seemed better than opening any fancy-wrapped present.

But even though I was excited to have the note, I was also scared. What if Carly was telling me off? What if she hated me now? A mean note from Carly? That would be more than I could stand. The ones from Maxine or whoever it was suddenly didn't seem so bad. At least they weren't from anyone who mattered to me.

As long as I didn't read the note, I could believe Carly was still my friend. I rubbed the paper between my fingers.

I wanted to feel whether the words inside were angry or apologetic, sweet or sour. But I couldn't tell. And as long as I didn't read it, I also didn't know if she'd forgiven me. I couldn't take it any longer — for better or worse, I had to know.

Amelia,

I have to admit you're right about Maxine. She does say mean things about you, but the way she does it, I'm not even sure it's nasty becuz she acts _to_ concerned — like "Poor Amelia! It must be awful to go around school in those horrible dork shoes!" See, she doesn't say you're a dork, just that your shoes are. Okay, this is a long way of saying that she did make me see you differently. But I don't judge people by how they dress. Just give me some time to figure out this Maxine thing.

Phew! SHE DIDN'T HATE ME! But what did Carly mean, she needed time to "figure out this Maxine thing"? Clearly Maxine was a vicious friend thief, trying to steal Carly. How could she not _see_ that? Or was she still deciding whether Maxine was worthwhile as a friend, even if she was a bad-mouthing friend?

That made me think. You can be friends with a person even when there are things about them you don't like. But there's a limit.

# GOOD FRIENDS

someone who gets your jokes — this is way more important than you might think

Someone who's honest with you and tells you stuff that isn't always easy to hear

someone you can do stuff with who likes the same things you do

someone who supports you, no matter how crazy your ideas are

# BAD FRIENDS

(ones where you keep wondering WHY you have anything to do with them)

**STOP IT!**

**I can't stand how you breathe!**

someone who is critical of you, always picking on <u>something</u>

**That's unusual.**

**And I don't mean in an interesting, exotic way. I mean in a "why in the world would you ever do that way."**

someone who thinks you're funny in a strange, odd way, not in a ha, ha way

**Really, what DO you see in her?**

**She's a total Loser with a capital "L." It's bad enough being in the same class as her — you shouldn't want to be closer!**

someone who bad-mouths your other friends

**I'd share, but I barely have enough for myself.**

**Oops, sorry! I guess I should have saved a place for you, but it didn't occur to me. I'm sure there's a seat in the back row.**

someone who won't share with you, even when they have PLENTY of whatever it is

someone who doesn't consider your feelings

I wish I could show Carly my good friend/bad friend drawings. She would laugh — we would laugh together. This is going to be a very long year if she decides she doesn't want to be my friend anymore.

It was hard, but I didn't call Carly that night. She asked for time, so I was giving her time. But I stared at the phone, willing her to call me. Every now and then, I checked the dial tone to make sure the phone still worked. It did. But no one called.

Ring, ring!

Come on, you stupid phone, do your job — ring!

I slept badly that night. In my dreams Maxine was cutting my hair, making me look really horrible. Carly saw me and screamed. She ran away before I could say anything. Then I looked in the mirror and I screamed too. That's when I woke up, with the snip-snip sound of Maxine's scissors still in my ears.

She turned me into a half-bald monster!

It was worse than the time I tried on makeup and ended up looking like a color-blind clown.

I tried to pick something cool to wear to school, but when it comes to clothes, I really am like a color-blind clown. I just don't get what makes something hot and something else NOT. Sometimes it seems like a fine line between the two. And sometimes what was cool yesterday is suddenly way UNcool today.

**COOL**

↑
lip gloss — especially flavored ones, like mango or papaya

**DORKY**

↑
medicated lip balm — the smell alone is enough to scream DORKY!

↑
flip flops — no matter how chilly it is, these are always in fashion — in fact, the colder, the better

overalls — NEVER in style unless you're a toddler or a farmer →

↑
tight, tight T-shirts — buy one size too small, then shrink in the wash for extra snugness

extraordinary large, shapeless sweaters — they look like you're trying to hide something — yourself!

I thought I looked okay, but I was nervous walking into science class. Carly was already there. She was too busy talking to Maxine to notice me. That was a bad sign. I couldn't hear what she was saying - she was practically whispering - but she didn't look happy. That was a good sign. Maybe they were having a fight. Maybe Carly was telling Maxine she never wanted to see her again. I could only hope.

All during class I kept trying to catch Carly's eye, but she wouldn't look at me. I wondered if I should write another note or if that would be bugging her, not giving her the time she asked for.

Not doing anything was horrible. Even if I didn't give her the note, I _had_ to write it, to do <u>something</u>. I tore a corner out of my notepad and started to write.

Carly—
I want to give you time like you asked, but it's HARD to wait. I need

That was as far as I got when a hand reached down and snatched up the note. I looked up, furious. And suddenly I wasn't angry at all - I was terrified. It was Ms. Reilly! I held my breath. Would she read the note out loud? I know that's what some teachers do when they catch kids passing notes.

"Don't read it, don't read it, don't read it," I chanted to myself. If she did, Carly would probably hate me forever for embarrassing her in front of the whole class. "Please, please, please," I begged in my head. If she didn't read it, I wondered if I'd get detention instead. For once I was rooting for detention. I'd rather have a year of that than lose Carly.

Lucky for me Ms. Reilly has a short attention span for anything that's NOT science. She forgot about my note and went on with the lab we were doing.

which falls faster? How does streamlining speed things up?

What I really wanted to know was how to make Carly move faster, how to hurry up her decision to get rid of Maxine. But I sure couldn't risk another note!

Ms. Reilly didn't say anything to me until the bell rang. Then she called me to her desk. I slunk up, waiting to be punished.

"Amelia," Ms. Reilly began. "You're a good student, so I didn't expect this from you. Normally, passing notes merits a detention, but I'll excuse you this once. This once," she repeated.

"It'll never happen again," I promised.

"I'm relieved to hear that." She handed me my note. "Here's your property back. Be more careful with your belongings in the future."

One good thing about Ms. Reilly taking my note was I was so worried about that, I forgot to be worried about Carly. Now I could put all my worrying back on her. I needed to talk with her, whether she'd had enough time or not.

I ran to the cafeteria to look for her. I hoped she'd be in our regular spot, waiting for me. She wasn't. I didn't see her anywhere, but I saw Maxine.

↑

Maxine was sitting next to some boy, trying to impress him with her oh-so-elegant lunch. Do boys care about stuff like that? I thought all boys cared about was how a girl looks. I didn't like Maxine, but I had to admit she was pretty — in a bland baked potato sort of way.

Anyway, if Carly wasn't with Maxine, I could finally talk to her. If I could find her.

I stood there searching for her, but I didn't see Carly anywhere. The cafeteria was crowded with kids, but I felt so alone. It was worse than being abandoned in a vast desert.

If I stayed there any longer, I'd get a reputation for being a total pathetic loser. I didn't want to become a cafeteria lurker— I had to sit somewhere.

I saw a place next to Leah and decided to grab it. She was still a friend even though she wasn't a close friend. At least she was several notches above an acquaintance and WAAAY better than someone whose face you recognize but you don't even know their name.

# FRIENDSHIP METER

← At the top — best, best friend: someone you talk to every day and can tell all your secrets.

← close friend: someone you spend a lot of time with, but days can go by without seeing each other.

← friend: someone you like, but don't go out of your way to be with. If they're around, fine. If not, that's fine too. Not close enough to trust with a secret.

← acquaintance: someone you don't like or dislike since you don't know them well enough to have an opinion. They're okay either way and someday might move up to friend status (or drop down to enemy).

← familiar face: you've seen this person before, maybe in class, maybe in the hall, but you don't know their name or anything about them except that they sometimes inhabit the same space as you.

← invisible: anyone in a lower grade.

← irritant: someone who bugs you, but not in a big way, more of a minor nuisance.

← enemy: someone you don't like and make sure that they know it.

← deadly enemy: someone you absolutely cannot stand. Even hearing their voice makes your skin crawl. If they're your partner on a project, WATCH OUT!

I was relieved that when I got closer, Leah called out to me to come over.

Hey, Amelia! Sit with us!

I forgot how nice Leah could be. Since we didn't have any classes together this year, I didn't see much of her.

"Would you look at that Maxine!" Leah said. "It's disgusting how she throws herself at that boy. Doesn't she have any pride?"

"You know Maxine?" I asked.

"Unfortunately." Leah scrunched up her face like she'd smelled something rotten. "I have English, social studies, and math with her — way too many classes. She's a stuck-up snob in all of them. All she cares about is impressing boys."

"Really?" That was a side of Maxine I hadn't seen. She was too busy trying to impress Carly around me. "I didn't know about that, and she's in my science class."

Leah laughed. "That's a good place for her. — who needs to build a Frankenstein monster when you have her? She's a scientific marvel, the heartless creature from the Black Lagoon."

"A monster? Because she likes boys?" That seemed harsh to me.

"No, because she's mean! Haven't you seen the vicious notes she writes? They're AWFUL! Talk about a poison pen!"

My stomach twisted. I was right — it was Maxine who sent me the nasty notes!

"Did she send one to you?" I asked. As bad as I felt, I was relieved I wasn't the only person Maxine hated.

"We've all gotten them." Leah turned to the two girls sitting on her other side. "It's kind of a club now — the nasty note club, courtesy of Maxine."

"I guess I'm a member too, then." I sighed.

"And I'm a member," said a familiar voice. I turned around — and there was Carly!

"She sent YOU one of those ugly notes!" I was shocked. "But she likes you!"

"That's what I thought too, but I guess not." Carly shrugged. "I suppose I was useful to her for a while. Until she got what she really wanted — a boyfriend."

she looked sad and exhausted.

Carly slumped down next to me.

I really thought she was my friend. Now I know she only wanted to be with me so she could get closer to my brothers — gross! When they weren't interested, she dropped me FAST! I feel like a tissue she used to blow her nose on, then wadded up and threw away.

"She wrote that I was a two-faced fake! Me, two-faced!"
Carly shuddered.

"Talk about two-faced!" I said and put my arm around her. It
was horrible that Maxine was mean to me, but I knew she didn't
like me. And I didn't like her. It was way worse for Carly. The
nasty note she got was more than mean — it was a betrayal, a
so-called friend turning into a definite enemy.

I wanted to do <u>something</u> to make Carly feel better. So I
said something I didn't really believe.

"Maybe it's not Maxine. We don't have proof she wrote
those notes."

"Oh yes, we do!" Leah was adamant. I <u>saw</u> her stick a
piece of paper into a locker. What could she be doing?
Returning notes she

borrowed or delivering

her <u>own</u>?"

Leah was all
fired up. There
was no stopping →
her now.

We should teach
her a lesson! We should
write the meanest, ugliest,
nastiest note of all and
stick it in HER locker—
see how SHE likes
getting that kind
of note!

Carly shook her head. "No. If we do that, we're as bad as
her. And that's something I NEVER want to be."

I liked Leah's idea, but I agreed with Carly, too. There must
be a way to give Maxine a taste of her own medicine without
stooping to her low level.

Suddenly I had it! → 🔆 The perfect revenge ← flashed in my head!

I told them my idea, and they loved it. Carly couldn't wait to get started, so we decided to be ready for action tomorrow. I almost felt sorry for Maxine — okay, not really, I didn't feel sorry for her at all. I was just eager to see her face once our plan was done.

I would love to wipe that smug smirk off her face. →

← And replace it with a sad, droopy mouth.

Carly met me after school, just like old times.

"I'm sorry, Amelia," she said. "I never should have listened to Maxine. I shouldn't have let her get to me."

"Yeah!" I agreed. "You shouldn't have!" I smiled at her. "But it's okay. At least you admit when you make terrible mistakes."

Carly shook her head. "I thought I was a better judge of character, but I guess Maxine fooled me because she looked so perfect."

"I know," I said. "She has to look that good to cover up how awful she is or no one would go near her. Talk about two faces! She has a zillion of them!"

When I got home with Carly, there was a note for me —
a postcard from Nadia!

Dear Amelia,
 Sorry to hear about the
new girl who's so mean. There's
a new girl in my class too, only
she's supernice. She's too nice
to pass any notes, good or bad.
Instead she taps her foot in
Morse code, but I can never
figure out what she's trying
to say. Oh well! At least with
words, you know what's going on.
( P.S. Remember when Twyla
tried to turn me against you? It didn't work!)

Yours till the note pads,
Nadia

304
Olives for Peace

Amelia
428 N. Homerest
Oopa, Oregon
97881

I'd forgotten about Twyla, but now that Nadia reminded me,
I could see her clearly — a tall, gangly girl who smelled like
sweet noodle pudding. She was always boasting about how
many friends she had because really she didn't have any. When
she tried to convince Nadia I wasn't worth having as a friend,
the plan backfired, and Nadia hated her for being a lying
creep. And, of course, she stayed my friend. Now it looked like
the same thing was happening with Maxine. It was weird
weird weird weird weird!
 ↖ This word just won't behave. It
    never looks like it's spelled right.

It made me wonder — is there something about ME that makes me an easy target for ugly comments? Is it my bad haircut? My lumpy clothes? My boring shoes? I had to ask Carly. Some things ONLY friends can tell you.

Carly, tell me the truth — are you embarrassed to be my friend?

Am I too uncool for you? After all, Maxine's comments would not have stuck if there wasn't some truth in them.

Carly thought for a while. I held my breath.

Well, there's SOME truth, you're right, but she WAY exaggerated things. I'm not proud of being willing to listen to her, but you know how important being cool is. Still, even MORE important than that is having a friend like you. I don't really care how badly you dress — it just gives me plenty of ideas of what to get you for your birthday.

Then she hugged me and we both felt MUCH better. "Now we have work to do!" Carly said, smiling. "We'll show that girl the power of the pen — let's get writing."

When we finished, we called Leah to check in with her. She was all set too. Tomorrow we'd meet at Maxine's locker before school.

I woke up excited to put our plan into action. I wanted to look perfect for once, so I snuck into Cleo's room and borrowed a shirt (she buys her own clothes with babysitting money and has MUCH better taste than Mom). I couldn't do anything about my hair or shoes yet, but it was a good start.

Carly grinned when she saw me. "Good going, girl! Nice shirt!"

I twirled around. "Compliments of Cleo!"

"Nice!" Leah agreed. "Now come on, before Maxine gets here."

We all headed for Maxine's locker. The hall was empty except for us. We couldn't help it — we cracked up as we slid the notes in.

I had to admit they were incredibly mean notes. I had to admit that we wrote them. But they weren't OUR words — they were Maxine's. Each of us had made copies of the nasty notes she'd sent us (since we'd all thrown away the originals). And I had to admit it felt GREAT shoving Maxine's ugliness back at her.

Now all we had to do was wait. It didn't take long. As she passed by, Maxine flicked her hair over her shoulder, barely nodding to Carly.

She ignored me and Leah, of course, twirled open the lock, and pulled open the locker. The notes tumbled out, a paper snowfall at her feet. I held my breath. Would she ignore them? Kick them away? Read them? Carly and I exchanged nervous looks. Leah bit her lip.

"Humpf!" Maxine snorted. Then she bent down and picked up a strip of paper. As she read, her lips twitched into a frown. She crumpled up the paper and threw it down, whirling around to face us.

"Did you guys do this?" she accused. "Think you're so smart—you're NOT!"

"What?" asked Carly. "You don't like getting your own notes? Now you know how it feels." She put her hands on her hips, defiant.

Maxine's lips trembled. For a second I thought she was going to cry. Then she snorted. "You are sooooo lame!" She grabbed her books and slammed the locker shut. "I don't care about your stupid notes. You just don't get it, do you?"

"No!" I snapped. "YOU don't get it!"

Maxine ignored me and looked straight at Carly.

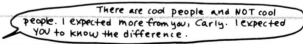

There are cool people and NOT cool people. I expected more from you, Carly. I expected YOU to know the difference.

"I do know the difference!" Carly's eyes flashed. "And I know just what group YOU belong to!"

Maxine rolled her eyes. "Whatever!" She stalked off, leaving an eddy of notes behind.

"I hate her!" Carly clenched her fists at her side.

I put my arm around her. "Come on, Carly, you're right — we know what kind of person she really is and she's not worth the paper she wrote on." I kicked the notes at our feet. "And she's not as tough as she looks. For a minute she almost cried."

"I saw that," Leah agreed. "She was almost human — almost. But she still doesn't know how to be a friend. She doesn't have a clue."

I put my other arm around Leah. SHE knew how to be a friend.

At lunch Carly, Leah, and I sat together. I didn't see Maxine and I didn't care. I was happy — for the first time in days.

"Look what I have in my lunch," Carly said, handing each of us a fortune cookie. "It's time for a good note — a lucky one."

I bit into my cookie and pulled → out the fortune.

You have friends who are loyal and true.

I didn't need a cookie to tell me that, but it's the perfect <u>note</u> to end on.

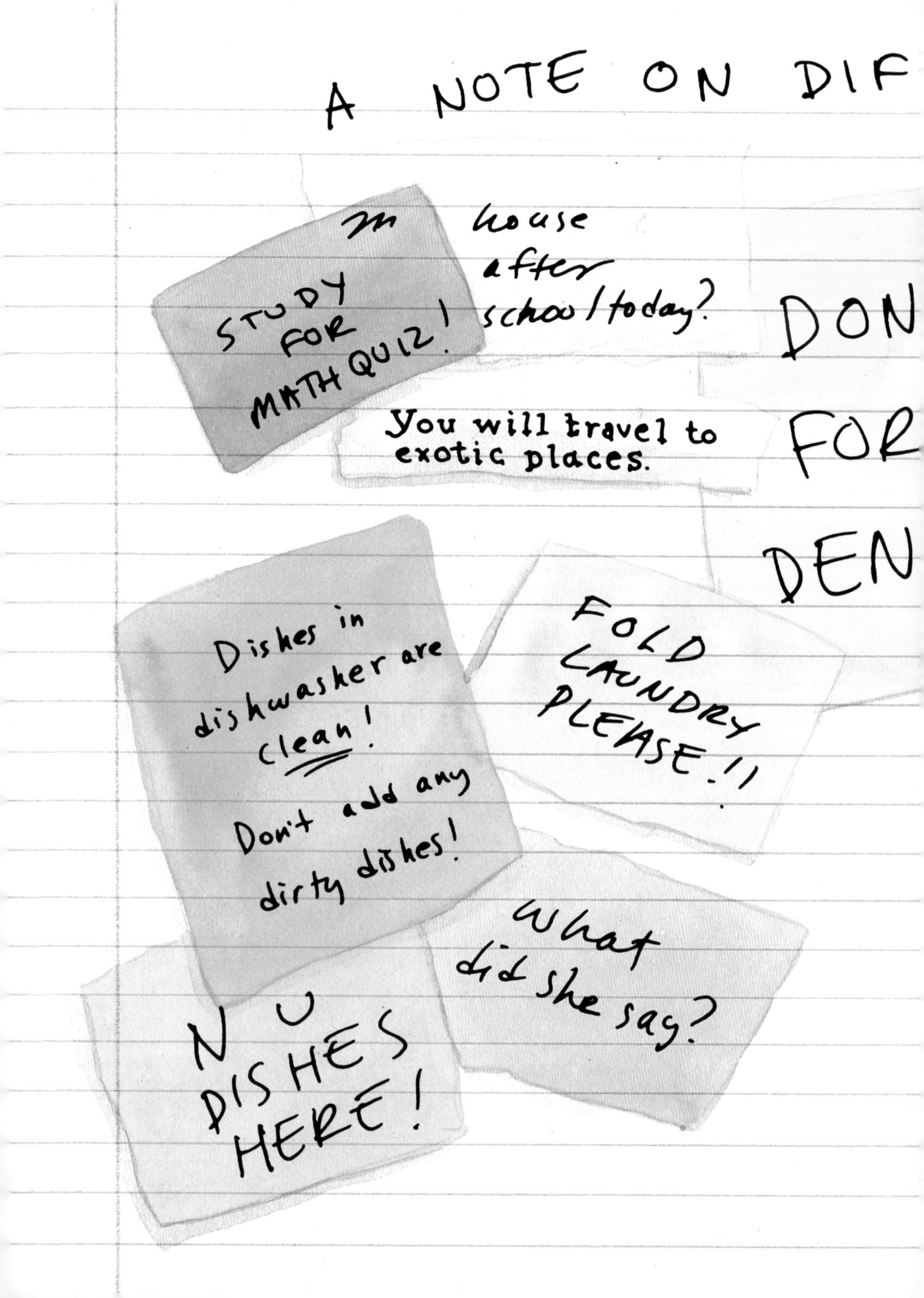

m

STUDY
FOR
MATH QUIZ!

house
after
school today?

You will travel to
exotic places.

DON

FOR

DEN

Dishes in
dishwasher are
clean!

Don't add any
dirty dishes!

FOLD
LAUNDRY
PLEASE.!!

N O
DISHES
HERE !

What
did she say?

ERENT NOTES

'T

GET

TIST

KEEP OUT!

At Carly's -
back for
dinner
(if it's a good
dinner)

Do you think
G. is cute?

What's the deal with words
that mean the same thing with
AND without a prefix?
flammable / inflammable
press/depress    ravel/unravel
valuable/invaluable
snare/ensnare  trap/entrap
canny/uncanny
tangle/entangle
part/depart
Are there more?  Why?

laundry
weed yard
3. homework
4. put back
nail polish
before C.
notices!

You owe me!

# a Note on What Makes a Good Friend

① Someone you can fight with and know they'll still be your friend.

② Someone who supports you even when you make stupid mistakes.

# BEST FRIEND RECIPE

① Take a person you like:

② Add 1 teaspoon respect
2 teaspoons curiosity
1 tablespoon shared interests
(things you like to do together)
a dash of a sense of humor
(makes everything work better!)
a heaping cupful of caring

③ Mix well and let sit for an hour.
Friendship takes time!

④ Bake to a crispy, golden perfection
and savor every bite!

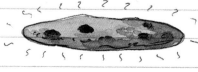

Friendship is like a fresh, warm cookie!

# Amelia's BFF*

Which one is it?

Can't it be plain and simple BFF?

* Best Friends Forever
Best Friends Fighting
Best Friends For Now?

by Marissa Moss

(and trying-to-be true blue friend, Amelia)

Nadia Kurz
61 South St
Barton, CA 91010

48¢

CAT'S GAME

Amelia
564 N. Homerest
Oopa, Oregon
97881

   Whenever I get a letter from Nadia, my old best friend before I moved away, it's like finding treasure in the mailbox. Sure, we email and instant message and post stuff on Facebook, but there's NOTHING like the excitement of holding a good, old-fashioned letter in my hands. For one thing, sometimes Nadia draws pictures. For another, her handwriting is like her voice — it tells me a lot about how she's feeling. Those aren't the kind of things a computer screen can show you.

Trust me, nothing can replace a letter!

I mean, who doesn't like to get mail?

Today's letter was extra, EXTRA, <u>EXTRA</u> special!
Nadia said she's coming to visit — <u>for one whole week!</u>
Her spring break isn't the same as mine, but her mom
said she can come stay with me and even go to school
with me.

IT'S GOING TO BE GREAT!!!

Nadia and I have been best friends for a long
time — like practically forever! We used to do
everything together. Trick-or-treating, sleepovers,
birthday parties, summer camp. Then I moved away.
But we've stayed friends thanks to the power of
letters, the occasional phone call, plus a visit every
now and then (like when we went to
Space Camp together).

↓

↑

Nadia and me as salt and pepper shakers one
Halloween. How cute!

I can't wait to tell Carly. She's my best friend close by, right here and now. I just know she and Nadia are going to love each other!

The three of us are going to have so much fun together! We'll be like the Three Musketeers — I can't wait!

Nadia          me          Carly

At dinner I told Mom about Nadia's visit. I thought she'd be surprised, but she already knew. Which makes sense once you think about it. Nothing happens without parents first talking things out and making decisions. Kids are the last to know what's going on, even when whatever it is has to do with us.

At least everything's all set now. Mom's even already talked to my school about having Nadia sit in on my classes for the week.

Unfortunately Cleo was also at the dinner table. Trust my sister to turn something nice into something nasty.

That's totally unfair! If amelia gets to have a friend visit, so do I! Or I should get to go stay with my old friends from our old place.

You're just jealous because none of your friends wants to see you— here or there. Do you even have a best friend?

Mom yelled at us to stop it. She said we should act our age instead of sticking out our tongues like babies. I can't help it. Being around Cleo is so INFURIATING I can't control myself. But I'd better. I don't want to get sucked into her stupid arguments when Nadia is here. I want everything to be perfect.

I wish I knew what makes Cleo SO annoying. Then I could develop an antidote for her, an anti-Cleo. I thought when she started high school she'd be better — or at least busier so I'd hardly see her — but she's worse. Now she's like exponential Cleo — Cleo x Cleo, bigger and louder than ever!

Carly's lucky. She has NO sisters, just two older brothers and they're both nice (and cute). She gets double goodness and I get Cleo. Yucch!

Marcus is 15 and one of the hottest - and coolest - boys I know. ↓

Malcom is 17 and gives Carly rides whenever she asks - lucky! ↓

At school the next day, I rushed up to Carly. I couldn't wait to tell her my news.

She could see something was up. ↓

What's going on? You look like you won the lottery. Has Cleo decided to move to Chicago to live with your dad?

Or did you win that art contest you entered? Did you happen to find a hundred dollar bill on the sidewalk?

"You're right," I said. "It is something great like winning the lottery or a contest."
"Well, what is it?"

You know Nadia, my old best friend in California before I moved here? I've told you about her — she's amazing! And now you'll get to meet her! She'll be here for a whole week! At my house and here in school, too!

You are excited. You're like a walking, talking exclamation point.

Sounds like you'll have a great time.

We'll have a great time! You're going to love her, I know it, and of course she'll love you. We can do all sorts of stuff together. It's gonna be so much FUN!

Strangely, Carly wasn't as excited as I thought she'd be. But then, she doesn't know Nadia — yet. Once she does, she'll see what a great week we're going to have, the best ever!

Carly may not have been excited about Nadia's visit, but she practically bounced out of her chair when Mr. Yegg, our social studies teacher, made his announcement.

Are you wondering why I'm wearing this hat and apron? Because it's time for the school-wide Bake-Off! Dust off your rolling pins and cookie cutters — you could win First Prize! And if not, you'll have a tasty snack.

If you want to buy one — all entries will be sold to raise money for the library and the winning baker gets a $50 gift card. Plus, I'm giving extra credit to every student who participates. So get cooking!

KISS THE COOK!

Carly passed me a note.

Let's look at recipes tonight. We're definitely gonna win — I can taste it!

Normally I only enter drawing or writing contests. I mean, I like to bake. Who doesn't? But I'm not particularly good at it. Considering my mom and Cleo are both disasters in the kitchen, that shouldn't be a surprise. But I know Carly's a good cook, so I guess with her help I can make something delicious. Better yet, Nadia will be here and she's a GREAT baker. She even makes her own bread! The three of us together are bound to win! I felt so confident, I passed a note back to Carly.

And Nadia can help us! She's the queen of cookies, brownies, and fudge and a master of flaky pie crusts! I'll tell her to bring her recipes.

Carly crumpled up the note and didn't look at me. Did I hurt her feelings somehow? I didn't mean to, but sometimes you can insult people without knowing it.

That extra weight looks so good on you.

Truly astonishing!

Wow! You're smarter than I thought!

I'm amazed you did that!

Didn't think you could!

At lunch I asked Carly if I'd said anything wrong.

"No," she sniffed. "I get it."

"Get what?" I sure didn't get it.

"I thought you wanted to enter the baking contest with me, but now I get it — you want to bake with Nadia."

I knew there was a misunderstanding!

"That's not it at all. I want to bake with both of you."

"Hmmm," snorted Carly. "I'm not sure I want to do that. I don't even know Nadia."

"Just give her a chance," I begged. "I know once you meet her, you'll be best friends, too."

Carly just took a big bite of sandwich and didn't say anything else.

I took a bite of dry, dusty sandwich and didn't say anything either.

I felt like I'd put my foot in my mouth, not my lunch.

I needed to do something to get back on Carly's good side. So I made a chart of cooking do's and don'ts — that's the kind of thing she likes.

When I showed my Do's and Dont's to Carly, she laughed. Now things are back to normal. Phew! Amazing what a little drawing can do. And I'm sure once she actually meets Nadia, it'll all be a piece of cake — one we bake together.

We can even invent our own kind. →

← Like instead of chocolate devil's food, why not cocoa friendship food? Sounds tastier!

Personally, I like devil's food.

That night I emailed Nadia about the bake-off.

"Bring ideas and recipes!" I wrote. She answered right away and said she's got lots of them. She's as excited as I am! I told her about Carly, Leah, Maya — she can't wait to meet everyone.

"And has Cleo improved with age?" she asked.

"Nope, the same old Cleo. Be prepared!" I warned.

"Anything else I should know about before I come?"

I couldn't think of anything. I didn't know I should have given her an entirely different warning.

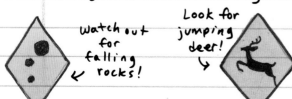

watch out for falling rocks! ←

Look for jumping deer! ↳

Oh, no! School ahead— with kids walking in the way! →

That made me think. Road signs tell us to watch out for stuff. Wouldn't it be nice if there were signs like that in life so we'd be better prepared?

↑
Dangerous crossing—
dog poop ahead!

↑
Person in a bad mood — do not talk to or approach!

↑
Fart coming—
do not inhale!

↑
Boring book —
do not read unless you want a nap!

↑
Windbag ahead — do not talk to unless you want to hear details about collecting jigsaw puzzles!

↑
Shower at own risk—all hot water used up by older sister!

Bad cook at work! →

Do not eat unless prepared ← for indigestion!

If there were really signs like that, I would have seen a big, bright flashing light.

APPROACH WITH CAUTION GO SLOW!

But of course I didn't. Life isn't like that. So I just made my plans for the bake-off and told everyone about Nadia until finally, FINALLY, FINALLY it was time to pick her up at the airport.

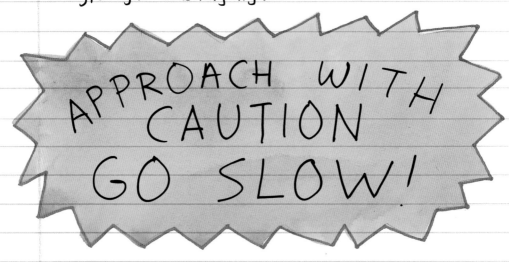

I've always wanted to get off a plane and have someone with a sign waiting for me. →

So I did that for Nadia. She loved it! ↙

NADIA

I guess part of me had been worried that she'd changed somehow, but she was exactly the same. I mean, she was taller and her face was thinner, and she wore a bra, but she was still the same old Nadia. Easy to talk to, fun to be with, smart, sweet, and sensitive.

Maybe she'd been worried about me, too, because she said how great it was to see me again, like we'd never been apart.

It was a perfect day. Even Cleo was nice. She can be — sometimes.

She gave Nadia a big → welcome hug.

Don't worry— I'll give you all the privacy you want. And I know you need the kitchen for baking, so I'll even limit my snacks.

Considering how Cleo loves to make big sandwiches, that was a nice offer.

The next day was Sunday, so we had all day to relax together before school started. We looked at recipes and talked a lot.

But there will still be some boring parts (like dull lectures) and annoying parts (like P.E.). I really owe Nadia as much fun as possible.

I tried to think of ways to make sure school would be entertaining. There's the bake-off at the end of the week, but what about all the days before Friday?

I could say it's my birthday and bring in cupcakes. I could ask the science teacher to demonstrate combustion again — explosions are always fun. I could bring in comics, bandes dessinées, for French. Comics in any language are great.

Or I could ask Carly to help me plan some fun things to do. I wanted to surprise Nadia so while she took a shower, I called Carly.

Amelia! I wondered if something happened to you. You haven't called all weekend.

Um, well, I've been kind of busy with Nadia.

She got here yesterday. That's what I'm calling about. I thought you might have some ideas how to make school fun for her.

Oh. Then there was a long silence.

"Carly, did you hear me?" I finally asked.

"Yeees," she drawled like she didn't want to answer.

"Well, any suggestions?" I asked again.

"Nope, sorry. After all, I don't know Nadia at all so how would I know what's fun for her?"

She had a point. Maybe after meeting Nadia on Monday, Carly would get some ideas.

"I guess you're right. You'll see her tomorrow and then you'll know. It'll be great!"

"Yeah, sure, great." Carly didn't sound excited, but after all, she didn't know what there was to be excited about — yet! She'd find out!

Nadia came out of the shower just as I hung up.

who were you talking to?

Carly. She can't wait to meet you! You guys are going to love each other!

Sure.

Nadia didn't sound so excited, either. Tomorrow would change ← all that.

I was excited enough for the three of us on Monday morning. When I saw Carly, I rushed up to introduce Nadra. Only it didn't go at all like I expected.

What I imagined.
↓

What actually happened.
↓

It was awkward and uncomfortable and not perfect at all.

Nadia didn't know what to think.

You said Carly was great. She seems stuck-up, if you ask me.

No, really, she's not like that at all. Maybe she had a bad weekend. Or she has some big project due. She's really warm and smart and funny. Give her a chance. You'll see.

But Nadia didn't see. First we had science — without Carly — but my next class was English with Ms. Hanover. True, there wasn't a chance to talk during class, but before it began, I tried to say hi.

Carly wasn't exactly warm or smart or funny.

Can't talk now. I've got to finish this.

In fact, I could swear she was giving me the cold shoulder.

The next two classes were okay because Carly wasn't in them, but then came lunch — a complete disaster. Nadia tried, she really did, but Carly either disagreed or ignored her. I'd wanted to make school fun for Nadia, but now I'd settle for bearable. What happened to make everything turn out so badly?

"Carly!" I was shocked. "What's going on? Why are you being so mean?"

"I'm not mean," she snapped, sounding pretty mean. She gathered up her trash and left. Just like that.

"Wow!" Leah rolled her eyes. "She's really steamed. What did you do to put her off like that?"

"I didn't do anything!" I protested. "And neither did Nadia."

Nadia looked miserable.

That made me feel terrible, like it was all my fault. Which I guess in some way it was, since Carly was my friend. I had to fix things. Now!

I put my arm around Nadia. "Carly's just in a grouchy mood. Tomorrow will be much better, so don't worry. She definitely doesn't hate you." Even as I said it, I desperately hoped it was true.

Leah looked at me like I was crazy. She'd never seen Carly so "grouchy" before. But I have. When I've made her mad. An angry Carly can be pretty scary.

"Anyway," I changed the subject. "We need to talk about the bake-off. We have to decide what to enter."

That cheered Nadia up. She loves to bake. So does Leah. They were talking about kneading technique, milk chocolate vs. dark chocolate, all kinds of details that meant nothing to me. I'm not a very sophisticated baker. I just know the difference between:

burnt          and          not burnt

And to be honest, I like burnt cookies and brownies. Nothing like a little carbon crunch.

Leah's much more picky. "I want to make something super special, something no one else can make."

"I agree," Nadia nodded. "It's risky, but if you get it right, it'll be spectacular."

Except I HATE messing up.

I want it all to be perfect! I can't help it – I have HIGH standards, I admit it.

"I'm just the opposite," I admitted. "I don't mind making mistakes so long as I get another chance to make things right. Maybe that's because I do make so many mistakes. I guess I'm used to it."

It's one reason I like to write — you can always rewrite stuff to make it → better. Too bad you can't rebake.

I wondered if I'd made a mistake with Carly, if I'd said or done anything to hurt her feelings. But Carly's always been clear — too clear — when I've done things before that upset her. She's NOT shy about telling me off.

Could I revise whatever made Carly mad? Too bad you can't redo things in life like you can in a notebook. You have to apologize and start fresh. Only I didn't know what I should apologize for.

My next class after lunch was social studies, another class with Carly. I didn't know how to make things better with her and I certainly didn't want to make things worse for Nadia, so this time I didn't even try to talk to Carly. I just introduced Nadia to Mr. Yegg, and we sat down together.

We're supposed to be studying Japan under the shoguns (same as Nadia at her school), but Mr. Yegg wanted to talk about baking.

Class, before we get to our samurai simulation, I wanted to talk a little bit about the bake-off from a historical point of view.

Have you ever wondered who invented baking? Who figured out that yeast makes dough rise? Who invented the chocolate chip cookie? Are there cookies in Japan or are they distinctly American?

I never thought about whether baked goods were part of our national culture, but maybe they are. After all, there's the expression, "As American as apple pie." I suppose the French equivalent would be "As French as croissants." For Italy, "As Italian as pizza." For Mexico, "As Mexican as tortillas."

Thinking about it, I was getting hungry even though we'd just had lunch.

As German as strudel.

As English as a scone.

As Dutch as waffles.

← As American as apple pie still sounds best.

For extra credit Mr. Yegg said we can write a page about the history of one particularly American bakery item, like buttermilk biscuits or cornbread. Then we'll get extra EXTRA credit if we bake enough of that item for the whole class to taste, plus give an oral report on it.

Nadia raised her hand.

I know I'm just visiting and not really in this class, but can I do a report on Parker House rolls? It's a great story!

Of course Mr. Yegg said yes — the more food for us to eat, the better! I'm proud of Nadia and I know she'll bake delicious rolls, whatever a Parker House roll is. I glanced at Carly. I thought now she'd see how great Nadia is, but she didn't look impressed. She looked angry.

In fact she looked so mad, I was afraid to go up to her after class or even after school.

Normally we walk home together but she wasn't waiting in the usual place. I was actually relieved not to see her. I didn't want a fight. I just wanted to have fun with Nadia.

It was a classic Nadia conversation. She's always full of these interesting tidbits of information. She should be on a game show.

For a while, being with Nadia was enough. I could forget how angry Carly seemed. But in the back of my head, a tiny voice kept reminding me.

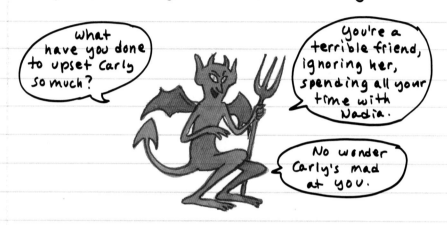

Was that the reason? I had to find out. While Nadia was busy writing her report on rolls, I called Carly.

I felt terrible. I hadn't ignored her on purpose, but somehow saying that wasn't enough.

"Look, Carly, I'm sorry. I thought you and Nadia would be friends, but you haven't been welcoming. I couldn't abandon her."

If I thought Carly's voice was cold before, now it was positively frozen.

"Why would I be friends with her? Just because you are? I think she's a little teacher's pet — and she's not even really a student here! How pathetic is that?"

I could feel my cheeks go red and hot. "She's not like that!" I yelled. "It was brave of her to talk in class like she did today. I think it's great she wants to do work even without getting credit. And the Carly I thought I knew would think so, too."

There was a long pause. I tried to think of the right thing to say, but my mind was a blank.

which door to pick?

↓

Apologize—
say you're
right, I'm
wrong. →

↑
change the subject.

Yell more,
get even
angrier,
she's wrong!
←

I could hear Carly thinking, too — and then a dial tone.

# CARLY HUNG UP ON ME!

No one's ever hung up on me before — it felt AWFUL! I was so upset, I was shaking. I wanted to call her back, but I couldn't. I just stared at the phone like it was poison or something.

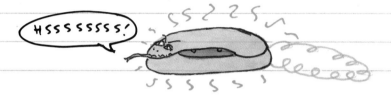

HSSSSSSSS!

I didn't want Nadia to see me like that. I didn't want her to have any idea what Carly said about her. So I sat at the kitchen table and took deep breaths, trying to calm down.

Cleo came in for her usual sandwich.

"You're not baking yet, are you?" she asked. "I'll make a snack later if you are."

"No, go ahead," I said. I was impressed she'd actually bothered to ask. Sometimes Cleo can surprise me that way.

"Is something the matter?" she asked. She was piling pickles, lettuce, tomatoes, cheese, and turkey on bread.

She was busy with her sandwich, but she still somehow noticed something was wrong. That surprised me even more.

So I blurted out what had happened.

"Wow," said Cleo between big bites of sandwich. "That's tough. Carly sounds really mad."

I know she's mad. I just don't understand why. I've tried to include her with Nadia. Trouble is, she's mean to her. I only started to avoid her after that.

Don't you get it? It's a classic BFF problem. You have two best friends. One close by — that's Carly. And one far away — that's Nadia. Which works fine so long as they're in their separate universes. Once you put them together, there's bound to be an explosion — a BIG ONE! With you stuck in the middle. After all, two's company, three's a crowd.

"Thanks for the cliché, Cleo," I said. "I don't buy it. Why can't they just get along? They don't have to be friends, but they can be friendly, can't they?"

"Just because you're friends with each of them, doesn't automatically mean they'll like each other. And chances are, they won't, because _you_ get in the way." Cleo chomped loudly.

"I do not! I'm trying to bring them together!" The more Cleo explained, the less everything made sense.

"C'mon, Amelia! Try seeing it from Carly's point of view. You shove this stranger in her face, tell her Nadia's her new friend, and P.S. you'll be spending all your time with Nadia for a week, so Carly'd _better_ like her."

When Cleo put it like that, it sounded terrible.

It reminded me of when we were little and Mom had a friend visit who happened to have a kid my age.

This is Felicity. You'll have a wonderful time together.

You're the same age — you have so much in common! Isn't that amazing!

I always felt like saying, "Yeah, me and about a zillion other kids. That doesn't make us instant friends."

I got it. I really did.

But I still think Carly could have talked to me if she was annoyed instead of acting so mean. After all, none of this was Nadia's fault. She was an innocent bystander. And was it really that ridiculous for me to imagine the two of them could be friends? Carly didn't even give Nadia a chance.

"So what do I do to fix this mess?" I asked Cleo.

"Talk to Carly. Apologize. Tell her you understand. But you also need to be prepared."

"Prepared for what?" She made it sound like I was facing a pit of snakes or bubbling quicksand."

Sometimes finding your way through a friendship feels like that.

↓          SSSSSSSS SSSSS
s

Burble, burble

"Prepared for Carly and Nadia simply not liking each other. It's hard when your friends don't get along. But it happens. And it's your job to make it work with each one of them."

I put my head down on the kitchen table. It sounded exhausting. Why is it so much work sometimes to be a friend? →

Just then Nadia came into the kitchen, grinning. Glad somebody's happy.

"I'm finished!" she said, waving a piece of paper. "I've done my report on Parker House rolls. Now can we bake some?"

That sounded like a great idea. Everything's all right when there's the smell of fresh-baked bread.

Things that turn any bad mood
into an instant good mood

cookies fresh from the oven

pajamas warm from the dryer

a purring cat

bare feet on sun-warmed grass

a hug from someone you love

hot cocoa

I felt so much better with a mouthful of fluffy, hot roll that I decided to call Carly back.

First I told Nadia what was going on, what Cleo thought, and how I was going to fix things.

Except Nadia didn't respond the way I thought she would. I thought she'd say yes, call Carly, if you tell her how much I want to be her friend, maybe she'll give me a chance.

She didn't.

The soft roll turned into hard rock in my stomach. Could it get any worse? Now Nadia doesn't like Carly and I'm the one stuck in between the two of them.

It was just like Cleo had warned me. This was supposed to be a great week, a perfect week, and it was turning into a perfect nightmare.

So I didn't call Carly. I couldn't with Nadia right there. And now it wasn't exactly friendly between us. It was cold and awkward. How did this happen? I used to have two best friends and now it looks like I have none.

I lay in bed thinking about how to fix things while Nadia watched a movie with Cleo — with Cleo!

↓

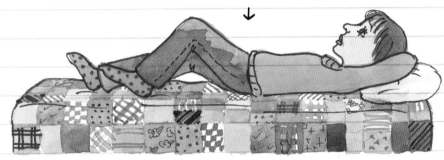

I wanted to call Carly to get her advice or write to Nadia the way I always do with my worst problems. But this time I couldn't, because they were both part of the problem.

I wasn't getting any ideas, so I decided to write a story in my notebook. That always makes me feel better, and at least I end up with something — a story.

# FIX-IT

There was a girl who was a genius at fixing things. She could make a broken piggy bank look like new. She could sew loose buttons on shirts. She knew how to patch a bicycle tire or a roof. She was as handy with a hammer as with a needle and thread.

People came from all over asking her to fix things. Some had fancy watches. Others had complicated machines with lots of gears and switches. One woman wanted her to fix her sick cat.

The girl took care of all of them, even the cat. She was proud of all her achievements and was sure there was nothing she couldn't repair.

Until one day three brothers came into her fix-it shop. They all looked very sad.

"You must have broken something very valuable," the girl said.

"We have," answered the oldest brother. "Each of us has a different problem. We've tried our best to make things whole again, but none of us has succeeded. We hope you can."

broken bits waiting to be made whole

"Of course I can," the girl assured them. "Show me what's broken."

The oldest boy told her how he'd lied to his best friend and now the friend couldn't believe him about anything important. "I've broken his trust," said the boy.

The girl frowned. "I can't fix that."

"Can you help me then?" asked the middle boy. He told her how he loved a girl and she'd loved him until she saw him kissing another girl. "I didn't mean anything, really. It was a stupid mistake! But now I've broken her heart," said the boy.

The girl shook her head. "No amount of tape or glue can fix that, and I can't, either."

"Then there's not much hope for me, is there?" asked the youngest boy. He described how he'd argued with his best friend and though he was very sorry, his friend couldn't forgive him for the mean things he'd said. "I've broken our friendship. Please help me fix it," begged the boy.

The girl sighed. "I'm sorry. I can't help any of you. Only you can fix those things, not anybody else. But you've given me something."

"You've shown me that not everything can be fixed with a little oil or a few stitches. There's only one tool I can think of to help you."

"What is it?" asked the brothers.

"Words. You need to find the right words to mend a trust, a heart, a friendship. And only you can know which words are the right ones."

The boys saw what she meant and went home to fix their broken pieces. Whether they found the right words or not, I don't know. But the girl had found a new tool to add to her collection — a notebook. Every night after she finished her repairs, she wrote in her notebook, looking for the right words for herself.

The End

After I finished the story, I knew what I had to do. No matter what Nadia said, I had to talk to Carly. And no matter what Carly said, I had to talk to Nadia. But first, I had to talk to myself. I had to be honest and admit that when I'd expected Carly and Nadia to be instant best friends, I hadn't been thinking about them.

I'd been thinking about <u>me</u>. I'd been selfish. And insensitive. I had to admit to Carly and Nadia what I'd done wrong, ask them to forgive me, and start all over again with what <u>they</u> wanted.

It was the only thing I could think of. It had to work.

When Nadia came to bed, I told her I was sorry about what happened with Carly.

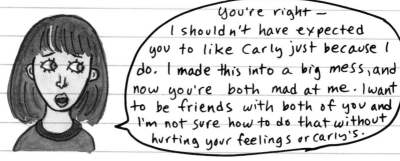

You're right — I shouldn't have expected you to like Carly just because I do. I made this into a big mess, and now you're both mad at me. I want to be friends with both of you and I'm not sure how to do that without hurting your feelings or Carly's.

There was a long silence. It seemed even longer because it was dark — a long, thick, dark, heavy silence.

I was afraid to say anything else and I thought Nadia had given up on me and fallen asleep. But she hadn't. I heard her sigh.

"It's okay, Amelia," she finally said. "You're in a tough situation, the kind of problem you would write to me about on a postcard. Only now I'm part of the problem."

"I thought the same thing!" I said. "I've missed asking for your advice — and getting it."

So now I'm imagining what advice I would give you if I weren't one of the friends you were caught between.

There was another silence, shorter this time and not so heavy.

"I don't know, Amelia. It's hard for me to say. Carly and I just don't get along. She clearly doesn't like me and I don't like her. That doesn't mean we can't be your friends, but it does mean you can't spend time with us together. You have to choose."

"That's impossible!" I said, "How can I choose?"

"I don't mean you have to stop being friends with Carly while I'm here, but at least don't eat lunch with her. Please? It's SO unpleasant!"

I sighed. Nadia was right. It was terrible.

"Okay, but give me a chance to talk to Carly about it. I need her to understand it's not forever, just for while you're here."

"Thanks!" Nadia said. "I feel much better."

"Me too," I agreed. Still, I worried about Carly. She might get really mad at me. Then what would I do?

All I could do was talk to her, try to use my words to fix things, and hope for the best. If I could get to sleep and tomorrow ever came.

I stared into the darkness for a long time. What if Carly decided I wasn't worth it, she didn't want to be my best friend anymore?

It was one of those nights where you only know that you finally fell asleep because you wake up. I didn't feel rested at all. At least Nadia was in a good mood. She had her Parker House rolls and report ready to bring to school. I hoped the snack would put everyone in a good mood, especially Carly.

At lunch Nadia sat with Leah while I talked to Carly.

What happened to Little Miss Perfect?

You mean Nadia? She's not perfect.

She seems to think so.

Look, Carly, that's what I wanted to talk to you about, this whole Nadia thing.

"Yeah, what about it?" Carly snapped.

"I'm sorry!" I blurted out. "I'm sorry I thought you'd like her just because I do. But she is my friend and she's staying with me this week, so I have to spend time with her." I swallowed the lump in my throat. "That doesn't mean you have to be with her, though. Maybe the rest of the week I should eat lunch with just Nadia. We'll have the rest of the year to eat lunch together."

Carly glared. "You're right that you shouldn't have assumed we'd be best buddies, but you're wrong to dump me to have lunch with Nadia. There's no reason we can't all eat together. I may not like Nadia, but I can be perfectly civil to her."

"You weren't yesterday!" I said.

"That was before you apologized. Now that you have, I promise I'll behave."

"Really?" I pressed.

"Really!" Carly insisted.

I had to trust her. What choice did I have? But since Nadia looked happy with Leah, I decided we'd start group lunches tomorrow.

← For now I tried to have a normal conversation with Carly, but it all felt clumsy and awkward. I wanted to go back to how we used to be. Had I ruined everything?

**BRRRING!** The bell rang and we all headed to Social Studies together. Nadia seemed happy after talking to Leah. Carly was quiet. So was I.

Mr. Yegg was thrilled to see Nadia with her rolls. They definitely put _him_ in a good mood.

Nadia, let's start class with your rolls. Pass them around and we'll listen to your report.

Nadia handed out the rolls along with the recipe and told stories about the Parker House Hotel. She did a great job.

## PARKER HOUSE ROLLS

This recipe works best if you have a large stand mixer → If you don't, beat the dough really well as you add flour. Nobody will ever make these as light and fluffy as my grandma, but every year, I try!

| | | | |
|---|---|---|---|
| 1 c. whole milk | 1/2 c. butter, melted | 1/2 c. sugar | 4 1/2 - 5 c. flour |
| 2 pkg. dry yeast | 1/4 tsp. salt | 2 eggs | more melted butter |

Warm milk in a small saucepan over low heat. Mix 1/3 of milk with yeast in a small bowl and let sit until bubbly, about 15 minutes. Put rest of milk into large bowl, add melted butter, salt, and sugar. Beat until sugar is dissolved. Add beaten eggs and bubbly yeast mixture. Add flour 1/4 cup at a time, using large stand mixer to beat at high speed. It should take 5 minutes to really beat flour well. When dough is too stiff to beat, stir in remaining flour by hand (if needed), enough to make a soft dough. Turn out onto a floured board and knead 5 minutes, until smooth and satiny. Place dough in greased bowl, turning over to grease both sides. Cover with a towel and let rise in a warm place until doubled in size, about 1 hour. Punch down dough and roll out onto floured board to 1/2" thick. Cut with 3" round cookie cutter (or use upside-down glass). Brush each roll with butter and fold in half. Pinch edge lightly so doesn't unfold as it bakes. Place in 2 greased 9" or 13" pans, cover with a towel, and let rise again in warm place until doubled in size, about 45 minutes. Bake at 350° for 20-25 minutes, until golden brown. Remove from pan and immediately brush with fresh melted butter. Now eat! Deee-licious!

I glanced at Carly. She looked interested — and she'd eaten all
her
roll.
←

After class Carly came up to us. "Nice job, Nadia,"
she said. "And you're a good baker. That roll was tasty!"
"Thanks!" Nadia's eyes sparkled like they do when
she's really happy. "And I'm sorry I've caused problems
between you and Amelia. Don't worry — I'll be gone in
a few days. You too, Amelia — stop looking so miserable
because I'm here."
"What? I'm glad you're here! I'm just worried, that's
all."
"Stop worrying," Carly said.
"Stop worrying," Nadia echoed.
I was so confused I didn't know what to say, but
the bell rang and we had to hurry or be late to French.
After school Carly wasn't at our usual place. That
seemed like a bad sign. Nadia didn't think so.
"Didn't you tell her at lunch that you needed to
spend time with me? She's just giving you that time.
Really, it's nice of her."
"I hope you're right," I said.
She was and she wasn't. As soon as we got
home, Carly called.

"What did Carly say?" Nadia wanted to know. I wanted to lie, but I didn't. I told her the choice Carly had given me.

"How can I do that?" I asked. "You're both my best friend. I don't want to hurt either of you."

"Look," said Nadia. "I'll make it easy on you — on ONE condition. I'm happy to bake with Leah. She already asked me, so I know she'll agree."

"Really?! You wouldn't mind?" I was so relieved, I felt like I'd just aced a horrible final exam. Then I remembered something she'd said. "Um ... what's the one condition?"

"I get to use our favorite recipe, the one for chocolate chip peppermint cookies. You and Carly have to bake something else."

It seemed like such a small condition, I should have been thrilled. But that's also Carly's favorite recipe. What if she insisted we bake them? I decided I would deal with that problem if it happened — later. At least the impossible choice had been taken care of.

"Thanks, Nadia!" I hugged her. "You're the best!"

"Remember that," she said. "I'm your <u>best</u> best friend."

And right then, she definitely was.

I called Carly back and told her I'd be baking with her, not Nadia. I could tell she was happy I'd chosen her — and that I'd decided so quickly.

"Guess that makes me your <u>best</u> best friend, huh?" she said.

"Yeah!" I squeaked. It was kind of true, in a way, maybe not that second, but still... I had to change the subject. "What should we make? How about some kind of pie? Mr. Yegg is big on pies."

"That's a good idea," she said.

"Phew!!" I thought.

Carly's going to ask her mom for a good pie recipe.

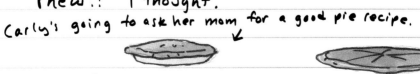

So many to choose from!

That was close! The pie suggestion worked —
Carly didn't even mention cookies. Yet. I wondered
if I'd survive this week. I had thought it would be so
much fun, but it was like walking through a minefield.
Avoid these dangers — step carefully!

GRRR

liver and onions—
P.U.!

← mean dogs

gum on
your shoe

Come with
me!

exploding
toilets

evil rats →

BZZZZZ

abducting
aliens

hungry mosquitos

Sniff!
Is that
me?

smelly
armpits

you're
late!

Jell-o with mystery
lumps inside

poison oak—
dangerous
itching
ahead!

overdue
library
books

Hi!

GASP!

bad breath

fighting friends

The next day at school, the four of us had lunch together,
Leah, Nadia, Carly, and me. We talked about baking and how
to make something that stands out from the crowd.

Leah said there are two ways to go — make something
classic that everyone loves and do a brilliant job. Or
figure out an odd combination that sounds like it wouldn't
taste good together, but turns out to be surprisingly
scrumptuous.

Like pineapple on pizza...

...or brownies with curry powder...

...or pumpkin butterscotch bars...

...or chocolate and peanut butter — a brilliant combination!

That seemed risky. You could end up with something gross,
like peanut butter and ketchup. Cleo used to like that!
Just because you like two things separately doesn't mean
they'll go well together.

Nadia disagreed. She said you have to be creative and
try new things. And some things are sure to taste great —
like peppermint.

Peppermint carrot cake? Peppermint oatmeal cookies?
I wasn't so sure. Carly said it's not peppermint, but
chocolate that makes everything taste better.

I wasn't sure about that either. Chocolate apple pie?
Chocolate prune danish? Yucch!

That made me think. Mixing friends can be like
mixing ingredients. Coconut doesn't go with tomato, mint
doesn't go with lemon. That was what happened
with Carly and Nadia — two great friends who
don't go together at all! If I think about them
like butterscotch and lemon, it makes sense!

Which I guess is why I need to try to keep them
apart. At least in the kitchen.

I showed Carly the recipes I'd brought, none of
which had creative ingredients. Chocolate mousse,
pumpkin cheesecake, and classic apple pie.

Her recipes were the opposite kind — the sort
with unexpected surprise ingredients like ginger or
pineapple extract.

We were so different, for a second I wondered
if we mixed well together. Maybe she wasn't
really my best friend.

Then I realized how silly I was being. Carly's a
better cook, that's all. We both agreed on one of
her recipes — pear pie with gruyere
crust. Gruyere is a kind of
cheese. Sounds strange,
but Carly
insists it's
yummy.

lemon merengue    chocolate cream          pecan      pumpkin

strawberry

I figured it was a good choice even though it sounded ~~weird weird~~ weird (like this word!) because I like making pies. And I love eating them.

After school, Nadia went home with Leah to bake and I went home with Carly.

And somehow being in the cozy kitchen, stirring and measuring, rolling out dough and slicing pears, we were back to being our old selves again, back to being simply best friends.

It was great.
↓

We joked and laughed like nothing had ever been wrong.
↙

The best part was once we'd finished. We rolled out the extra pie crust and made honey pies with the scraps. We couldn't taste the finished pear pie since we had to enter it into the bake-off, but at least we could eat the honey pies—yum!

How to make a honey pie: roll out the extra dough, smear with butter, cinnamon, and sugar. Fold over into a pocket. Press edges with a fork to seal. Bake and eat while warm!
↙

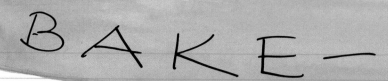

# BAKE-

Baking factoid:
The first cookies were used as oven testers. Bakers would put a spoonful of cake dough into the oven. When the dough was crisp, they knew the oven was hot enough to bake in. And so the cookie was born!

Mama!

The day of the contest, the whole school smelled great! Not like rubber balls and white board markers, but like chocolate, cinnamon, licorice. Everything looked delicious. I wished I was one of the judges so I could taste it all. Lucky Mr. Yegg and Ms. Li got that job.

"Your pear pie looks amazing!" Nadia said. "I always have problems getting the crust to look pretty."

"Thanks," said Carly. She deserved all the credit for how well our pie turned out. If I'd made it alone, it would have been a Frankenstein pie.

"Your cookies smell wonderful," Carly said. "That's my favorite recipe, too."

I stared at them. If I didn't know better, I'd say they were acting like friends. Maybe it was all the good smells they were breathing in.

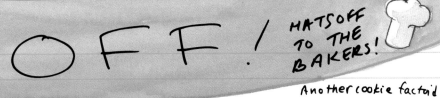
# OFF! HATS OFF TO THE BAKERS!

There were so many desserts to choose from, I didn't think we had much chance of winning. So I wasn't too disappointed when Eli won first prize for his dark chocolate mousse.

"We could have made that," Carly whispered to me. "I should have listened to you — classic beats oddball every time."

"Not every time. And then we wouldn't have made honey pie — that was worth more than a prize."

"Maybe," Carly said. "But I like to win."

I laughed. "I'd rather eat!" Now that the judging was over, it was a regular bake sale. I bought slices of pie for all of us to try. Yummy!

m m m m m m m m m m m m m m m m m m m m m m!

We each bought something different and traded tastes.
It was a bakery feast — and a sweet way for
Nadia to end her visit.

The next day we drove her to the airport.
"It wasn't what I expected, but I loved having
you here," I said. "You'll always be my best
friend, no matter what!"
  "Yeah." Nadia smiled. "You've proven that!
It's cool that we can grow and change and still
be friends. I've outgrown other friends — not
you." She hugged me. "Next time you come
see me. Maybe that'll be easier."
  I nodded. Somehow I imagine it won't be,
but it won't matter, not one bit. We'll deal
with it.

I have faith we'll stay friends. →

No matter what. ←

Then Carly came over and it was like Nadia had never been here. No more tension, no more ruffled feathers, just me and Carly, best friends, baking together.

This time we made our favorite cookies, even better than honey pie.

And that's what makes true best friends.

# Amelia's Notebooks

write on! ↓

I've written 25 26 notebooks! Which is your favorite?

Read on! ↓

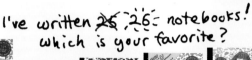

I wish I could forget them!

← Pssst! Did you hear the one about Mr. L?

The good, the bad, and the totally freaky!

← Carly's favorite so far!

Plus all <u>these</u> from elementary school ↓

The first and original! →

↑ Still my favorite!

There's lots more info and fun stuff at marissamoss.com and KIDS.simonandschuster.com. Even a <u>real</u> Amelia movie!